RISKY BUSINESS

A sudden sound in the distance caught TC's attention. He stepped away from the shower stall and looked off to the south. What he saw suddenly gave him an idea.

"The Marauders will be on the move. We're going in pursuit. It's my intention to destroy the MBT's if we can't recover them intact."

Falken had already figured that out. "That'll mean the end of Armbrust."

TC grinned. "Not necessarily."

Falken looked at him quizzically. "What do you have in mind?"

Creighton pointed to the southeast. A gray haze stretched across the horizon.

"We'll need Shona and Telfi." Creighton then explained his plan. When he had finished, Falken looked at him incredulously.

"It'll be risky," said the IFV commander.

"We're in the business of risk."

★★★★★★★★★★★★

Also by Bill Dolan

AFRIKORPS

Published by
HarperPaperbacks

BILL DOLAN

AFRIKORPS

IRON HORSE

HarperPaperbacks
A Division of HarperCollins*Publishers*

This is a work of fiction. The characters, incidents, and dialogues are products of the author's imagination and are not be construed as real. Any resemblance to actual events or persons, living or dead, is entirely coincidental.

HarperPaperbacks *A Division of* HarperCollins*Publishers*
10 East 53rd Street, New York, N.Y. 10022

Cover illustration by Danilo Ducak

First printing: November 1991

Printed in the United States of America

HarperPaperbacks and colophon are trademarks of HarperCollins*Publishers*

10 9 8 7 6 5 4 3 2 1

For Gary Gardner, whose father
doesn't believe we're neighbors!

★★★★★★★★★★★★★★★

Prologue

★★★★★★★

2050.

Dr. Carl Eliason was tall, blond-haired and had blue eyes that sparkled from within a richly tanned face cultured from hours of walking the New Mexico desert. He had once spent hours walking what seemed an endless place of sand; a place where he found the solitude and open space the best therapy for a mind tortured by the reality that was now approaching faster than anyone could comprehend.

It's actually happening! he had to remind himself.

Sitting four levels beneath another desert, he thought of the responsibility he and others had accepted. The ramifications. It was the act of cowards, some might say. They might say that if anyone else ever found out about their plan, other than the eight hundred within the complex.

He was listening through a headset to the satellite transmission between one television station in Tokyo, and another station in Atlanta. The man in Tokyo was in a panic.

"Tokyo is almost gone," said the voice, which rang with the special fear of a man who finally recognizes that he was wrong. Deadly wrong. "The dikes have ruptured. The city is flooded. A wall of water has killed millions. Their bodies are gone forever. In a few hours, Tokyo is gone forever. I fear . . ."

The transmission ended.

Eliason switched off the radio, settled back into his chair, and allowed himself the last true luxury of this lifetime. He lit a thick, pungent Cuban cigar. He drew in heavily, blew a cloud of blue smoke, and watched the cloud turn gray, then yellow, and finally red as the smoke drifted against the bright lights burning from the computerized console filling the wall of the control center.

The Living Room, it was called. Truly, a living room. A room where the lives of the living would be controlled for the next century. Or destroyed, if there wasn't proper maintenance.

That would be the task of the Sentinels. The Sentinels were the people selected to monitor the sophisticated life-support systems over the next one hundred years. Or longer, if necessary. Many would awaken in the future, work for five years, then return to a restful sleep. The lives of hundreds would be in their hands.

Twenty members would work each five-year shift. Those one hundred were selected by drawing lots; only the children were exempted. Instructions were clear to all the Sentinels; they understood the revitalization process necessary to awaken the next group of Sentinels. Each understood the processing method to return the previous Sentinels to their deathlike sleep.

All were trained. All were ready. The time had come.

Earth was dying.

Cataclysm!

The complex had taken ten years to construct. Ten years in secret in the desert; bribing government officials, storing food, installing the equipment needed to ride out the coming century of earth's hibernation.

Hibernation? Wasn't that what they would do? Hibernate. Sleep through the long winter they had so often predicted. Had their efforts not failed, who knows? Perhaps. . . .

He sat up as Phillip Chan entered. Phillip was a short man with large eyes that seemed to move constantly. He was from Singapore. A nuclear physicist, he had learned of the *Prometheus* Project from his brother, a member of the United Nations Weapons Reduction Committee.

Weapons reduction! Indeed. A good idea for the wrong reasons. And too damned little, too damned late.

"Good evening, Carl." Phillip sat down and gazed at the control console. He saw the cigar and chuckled. "Those things are bad for your health. Or didn't you know that?"

Both men laughed. "I may as well take some remembrance of the past with me. There'll be none of this left when I return."

A long pause followed. "You have your instructions?"

Phillip nodded. "You know the emergency list for your watch?"

"I do. But I doubt it will be necessary. We are all trained well. There are manuals for every contingency. Besides, this place is built so well . . . it'll outlast us all." He opened a folder with a list of names of people who were to be awakened during his shift in the event of specific problems. The list included electricians, concrete specialists, structural engineers. Every conceivable form of craft was at his fingertips. All he had to do was press the right button and within a few hours whatever specialist he needed would be awakened.

"Let's hope you're right. I don't like being awakened from a deep sleep."

Another pause, then both men burst into laughter; laughter that was followed by a stream of tears from each man's eyes.

"Oh, God, Phillip . . . how did this happen?"

"It was our fault, Carl. There are no others to blame. We are the ones ultimately responsible for earth. We were her caretakers . . . and we failed. Failed miserably, I might add."

Carl reached into the drawer of the desk and removed a bottle of scotch whiskey. Aberlour.

"How about one for the road?"

Phillip's eyes narrowed. "Do you think that's wise? You're to be processed. The alcohol might cause a distortion."

Carl harumphed. "Distortion. In some ways I don't care. I don't know if I want to be here when this concrete sardine can is opened. Who knows what we'll find. If there is anything to find."

"The biosphere inhabitants," he reminded Eliason. "There will be someone left to carry on."

"Biospheres. I hate the thought of people sitting through the Cataclysm in their glass fortress. It would be like watching a hundred-year blizzard through the living-room window. No night. No day. Nothing but . . . nothing."

The mood became more somber. Phillip asked, "I wonder what they'll be like?"

"Who?"

"The biosphere inhabitants. The 'specials.' I wonder what they'll be like. Imagine, generations of people with no contact with the outside world."

"Like the shrimp in the Arizona Concept."

Both men laughed. The laughter felt good in this place where there was nothing humorous.

"A world in a bowl," said Phillip. "You did solve one

of the problems though. An important problem the original biosphere didn't consider. At least, not in its long-range plan."

"The water," said Carl.

"The water."

"Odd, isn't it. The entire concept was based around a tiny shrimp. A glass globe was built. Water was poured into a hole. A shrimp was placed inside, then a piece of seaweed. With the right amount of sunlight, the ecosphere would survive."

"Yes. But people aren't shrimp. People can't live submerged."

"They won't have to. They have the perfect re-creation of an ecosphere:

"*Earth.* The sand, gravel, and soil needed at the base of the sphere.

"*Air.* The sphere will thrive on the oxygen created by the biomes.

"*Fire.* The sunlight will provide the energy that will sustain the life. Christ. There will be sunlight. Especially when the ozone layer is totally depleted. Sunlight like never imagined. But the filters built into the glass will eliminate the harshness. They won't burn to a crisp.

"*Life.* There will be life. Procreation of human and plant life. They'll survive. We saw to that. We have nothing to be ashamed of, dear friend."

Phillip laughed facetiously. "Yes. But it was the water. That was the key. The shrimp live in water. Humans don't."

Carl felt a certain pride in the accomplishment. "Yes. Water. The Arizona Concept is a world of air . . . not water. People aren't shrimp. People breathe air. That was a good contribution."

A strange sadness came over Phillip. He had seen this coming for decades. He had stood on the mountaintops of political power and shouted the warning, but no one listened.

"I expect they'll be nothing but robots in the end. People without character. Life shapes character. There'll be no life. Only . . . survival."

"They'll be a strange lot, I suspect. But I'd predict they won't be the type to make the same mistakes we made. They'll be different. They'll be virginal, in a sense. Imagine . . . a new world waiting. A world they have to sit and watch inch its way back into their possession."

"It will be horrible."

"A nightmare."

Phillip checked his watch. "Speaking of which . . . I believe it's time for your Rip van Winkle act."

Eliason drained the last of the scotch. He put the bottle away, and said, "The next time I see this, it'll be the oldest scotch on the face of the earth."

Carl went to the door. Phillip followed. They embraced, then shook hands.

"So long, old friend," said Eliason. "I'll see you in a hundred years, give or take a decade or two."

"We'll have another drink."

Eliason acted as though there were more he had to say; then, he realized there wasn't. He had said it all. They all had.

He walked to the elevator and rode to the fourth level. The wall was filled with booths. In each booth there was another human being. Each waited in deep, frozen sleep. Waited for the Cataclysm. Waited for the end of the world. Waited for the fresh new world.

He stepped into the booth marked with his number. Then he paused and stepped outside again. With a small penlight he flashed the beam through the glass plate of the door sealing the adjacent booth.

His wife sat in serene sleep. Her blonde hair was hidden beneath the protective helmet. Behind the helmet's faceplate her face was covered by the thin suit of material that sealed the rest of her body. She looked like an astronaut ready for flight to a distant planet.

In a sense, he realized, she was. He kissed the glass of the door, then turned to the other door beside his chamber.

Another of his loves sat in a reclined seat. She was younger. Her blonde hair and blue eyes were covered like her mother's.

He stared for a long moment at her. Knowing his young daughter was medically dead made him shudder. Knowing she would be brought back to life made him optimistic.

After a long while, he went into his capsule. He slipped on the protective outer skin, then climbed into the suit and placed the helmet over his head, sealing the locking track of the helmet into the neckpiece of the suit.

When locked in, he slipped on his gloves, then reclined in his seat. He adjusted the harness that would hold him in the seat, no matter what his body tried to do. The release could only be activated by a Sentinel. They were all designed that way.

He sat and emptied out his final thoughts, then pressed a button on the side of the seat.

The door sealed. There was the sound of air being pumped from the room. He grew lightheaded, then heard the sound of the freezing mist entering the room.

He grew cold. Terribly cold, then began gasping for breath and felt the instinct to fight. The straps held. More lightheadedness followed, then giddiness as he was slowly rendered unconscious.

In his mind he saw a burst of light. There was a

lighted path. He saw himself running. His child was at his side. His wife followed.

They ran . . . ran . . . along the lighted path . . . then disappeared . . .

Into the next century. Into the new world.

PART ONE
THE MAGI

★★★★★★★★★★★★★

Chapter One

★★★★★★★

Colt Derider descended from a long line of adventurous Americans; Americans who enjoyed building things, not blowing things up. Derider was an engineer; on his personnel file the background information summarized his life as the following: engineer, surface transportation, locomotive (electric and/or solar-powered.)

How he had wound up in Quadrant One, Africa, as the resettled territory of North Africa was now labelled, was a mystery he continued to ponder. Four months ago he was in DESFOR, the Western Quadrant, United States. He was building a railroad; one of many now stretching across the pacified country. His track was running from the Omaha Biosphere to the Vegas Biosphere, by way of Salt Lake and Carson.

Like his forefathers before him, Derider loved trains, especially the old steam locomotives, though outdated and no longer considered in any sense other than historical. Visions still filled his head of his ancestors: Parren Derider, the surveyor for Grenville Dodge during the 1800s when Dodge was building the Transcontinental Railroad. Or Parren's son, Colt, his namesake, who carved the trail through the steaming jungle of Panama, linking the two great oceans before the building of the Canal.

Tough, hearty men. Men who faced danger, as had

the Deriders, who later travelled in the same footsteps as their forefathers.

In 2050, Colt's great-grandfather was the only true expert on trains in the United States, a distinction that began with his selection as the "special" who would enter the Omaha Biosphere at the beginning of the Cataclysm. The Derider talent would survive in order to one day rebuild a network of silver ribbons linking the nation.

But Africa? Jesus Christ! A track was already running east from Base Camp One in the Quadrant. Now it was time to begin the run to the south. The proposed area had to be surveyed before the actual laying of track began.

Which meant he had to go into hostile territory under the protection of soldiers of AfriKorps. Soldiers trained in desert fighting. Soldiers who instinctively knew when there was cause for alarm.

And now there was alarm.

He felt the warm breath of the soldier next to him as the man whispered, "You sit tight and keep your eyes on that thermal imaging screen. I'm going to slip out the bottom and work around their rear. If you get movement . . . hit this switch."

Lieutenant Reno Falken was sitting in one of the two seats in the command cupola of his infantry fighting vehicle, pointing at a switch on the instrument panel. The switch was marked FLARES.

Derider didn't know much about military equipment, but he was familiar with the thermal imaging screen. The heat sensed by infrared sensors in the night would separate various heat signatures into distinct color patterns according to their temperature. Set at the human range, heat between ninety-eight and one hundred degrees Fahrenheit would appear blue.

Which meant the image was an intruder.

Derider nodded, then looked seriously at the young soldier; a soldier he had come to know and admire since arriving from the United States.

"Be careful, my boy," a voice laced with sincerity and great concern warned from one of the seats in the rear of the IFV.

Roman Standish, the philosopher and teacher, who often served as negotiator, looked severely at Falken. The man looked like a modern-day version of Socrates, with his long white toga, his leather sandals, and flowing white beard. Roman sat in one of the webbed seats lining the interior of the IFV. He looked as out of place as Derider felt.

Kneeling at the hatch in the floor, Falken winked at Roman, lifted the cover, then dropped into the warm sand beneath the vehicle.

Quickly, Reno's mind flashed a schematic of the area. His IFV was sitting at the edge of a plateau overlooking a deep valley. The survey team had been three days on the plateau and adjacent area, mapping the route the new "roadbed," as the engineer called the foundation on which the tracks would be laid and the train would one day run.

Trains. Reno knew little about trains, except the one to which he had seen stationed at Base Camp One. The train arrived in sections and had been assembled in what was called the "roundhouse." The train looked like a bullet and carried an awesome array of weapons.

The personnel of AfriKorps had called the train the "Iron Horse."

Falken liked Derider, who talked about trains, tracks, and roadbeds the way soldiers talked about food, sleep, and moist pussy.

Then he cursed his luck. Or the timing. Either way, he was sitting with an IFV parked near the ledge with three Marauder tanks bivouacked near the only avenue of withdrawal from the ledge.

His team had not yet been spotted by the Marauders, which he figured was a probing unit moving up from the south. The Marauders had taken a good ass-whipping a few months ago shortly after the arrival of the AfriKorps, a multinational armored force composed of American and European military units ordered to "stabilize Africa" and rid the continent of the horde of approaching Marauders sweeping from the south to the European Continent. Contact had been limited since that earlier engagement, until now. And if he was right, the Marauders were mounting another penetration campaign.

Which presented a pressing and disturbing dilemma: his IFV couldn't go forward, since the Marauders would hear it and probably blow it to bits; or retreat, unless he could figure out a way to make the IFV fly.

And Colonel Clayton had been specific: "If anything happens to the engineer . . . I expect the same to happen to you!"

Carefully, he slithered along the hard, rough ground until he reached a stand of boulders near their escape route. From beyond, the sound of voices filtered through the air; coarse voices, speaking in a language he didn't understand.

From around his neck he pulled up his NVG, night vision goggles, adjusted them tightly against his eyes, and checked his armaments.

He carried an automatic assault rifle with uranium depleted bullets; the bullets would penetrate body armor and the armor of a tank. On his harness were five high-intensity thermite grenades, each capable of raising the temperature within a twenty-foot radius to over 5,000 degrees Fahrenheit, or if dropped through a turret, melting a tank as though it were butter. Or turning a human being into ash within seconds.

Getting close would be the trick, and mulling this thought over, he was surprised—stunned—to see the Marauders were beginning to make his decision for him.

Through the darkness a green-white figure appeared, turned the strange color by the starlight effect from the NVG. The figure stopped and began relieving himself beside where Reno lay in the rocks at the base of the boulders.

The smell of urine stung Reno's nostrils; the acrid burn of the waste splashed off the ground, formed a stream that ran under his armpit and pooled against his camouflage fatigues.

Reno waited, and when he felt the man shaking himself, he stood up and ran a razor-sharp knife through the Marauder's carotid artery.

There was only the slightest struggle, then the sickening gurgle from air mixing with blood, and the man slumped to the ground.

Reno took a thermite grenade and pulled the pin; in his other hand he gripped the assault rifle. His finger switched off the safety switch and he stepped forward, hoping the Marauders would think he was their man returning from taking a leisurely piss.

Three men sat around the fire; looking like ghouls against the flame licking the night air.

The first looked up, a surly, ill-clad varmint Reno recognized as a nomad from one of the tribes recruited by the Marauders.

The man started to shout, but Reno's first bullet tore through the man's upper jaw, then blew off the roof of his skull.

Running, Reno dropped the thermite grenade and dove for the nearest of the three tanks. The explosion turned the desert into what could only be described as Hell.

Two more Marauders were consumed by a cocoon of white-hot flame, wrapping their bodies tighter in the fiery grip as they twisted and danced through the small tornado of fire swirling near the campfire.

Reno was on the tank, dropping another grenade through the turret. Then he fired from the hip as he jumped clear, killing another Marauder who was coming out of the second tank. A flick of the wrist and another thermite grenade was ready; in the next instant the tank was buckling from the intense heat melting the inside of the armored unit.

The third tank had buttoned up and had the engine turning over as Reno ran in pursuit. The tank was nearly reaching the darkness at the point where the black of night was gray against the white of the roaring thermite storm.

The turret turned, and he saw a coaxial machine gun training on him. Diving, the bullets stitched the hard ground, swept innocently past him, and etched the night with the tracer signature, marking the bullets' path.

Quickly, Reno removed a grenade from his harness. The long, cylindrical grenade was thrust onto the muzzle of his assault rifle, and was now ready for launch.

That's when the tank suddenly lurched, then spun wildly to the right and appeared out of control.

Reno steadied the weapon on the tank but didn't fire. For some reason, he felt unthreatened.

The grinding of the treads squealed as the tank turned on one track, then jerked in the other direction, as though being steered by a drunk.

The tank sat motionless; behind him, the thermite firestorm was receding. Within the next minute the darkness had returned; the area was silent, except for the fuming and buckling of the burning tanks.

Reno knelt, watching. Waiting.

He started to rise when he heard a sound from behind. Whirling, he levelled his weapon on a strange figure approaching through the eerie light; framed against the fading firestorm was a man wearing a flapping shroud.

"Roman. Damn you. I almost shot your ass off!" Reno snapped.

Roman Standish marched undaunted toward the young soldier. Through the haze and smoke, Reno saw Derider appear.

"So this is what it's like," said Derider, looking with a sick expression at the crumple of burned flesh lying on the ground.

Reno nodded at the dead Marauder. "Your first time?"

Derider nearly vomited, and the question was answered by the disgust on his face.

Reno took a communicator from his harness and spoke quickly into the walkie-talkie. "Bring up the IFV. Let's un-ass this place. ASAP."

The driver's voice crackled over the headset, and Reno swept his arm toward the stalled tank.

"I don't know about that one. I think it's still active." He raised his weapon and started to fire.

"No!" shouted Roman. He was pointing at the tank. "Look. Look at the turret."

The turret was open. Standing in the turret was a small figure. Reno approached carefully, slipping his NVG's over his eyes to give full clarity.

As he neared the tank, he stopped. Roman's voice again spoke, this time at his shoulder.

"It's a child."

Reno pulled down the NVG's. In the turret stood a small child. A girl.

Reno had never seen anything like the child in his life. He had seen filthy hostiles in DESFOR; raggedy-assed nomads in Africa, but nothing like this.

The child said nothing. She only stared.

Reno shined his flashlight on the child. "Christ. Look at what's on her head."

The child was dressed exquisitely in what appeared to be a dress of gold. She shimmered as she stood in the turret. On her head was a crown; jewels encrusted the crown.

But the most unique feature was her face. Her skin was black; black as the night. Her hair was white; white as moonlight. Her eyes appeared red; red as the blood coating the blade of the dagger in her hand.

A trail of blood dripped from the dagger, running into the webbing between her fingers.

Roman leaned and whispered to Reno, "We had better send for Shona."

"Who's Shona?" asked Derider.

Reno turned slightly, keeping his eye on the child as he talked to the engineer. "Something of a mystic. A desert guru. He knows all the people in the area. I think you're right, Roman. But we can't stay here. We can't wait. We have to get the hell out of this area. This could be a recon unit. A larger element could be *en route* right now."

Roman nodded, stepping closer to the tank. He reached up his hand, saying, "Come, child. We won't harm you."

The child touched her white hair, then looked at the white hair of Roman Standish.

Carefully, with an elegance, and even grace, the child

climbed down from the tank. At the edge she was hoisted down by Roman.

"Who is she?" whispered Reno. He was looking at Roman.

The strangest look was on the face of Roman Standish. When he replied, the infantry officer looked at him dumbfounded. He thought he heard right, but wasn't certain. He asked again, this time while looking at the child.

Reno felt the child's eyes; they seemed to penetrate to the soul. A calming came over him. Then he heard Roman repeat himself, and wondered if the old man had lost his sanity.

"She doesn't appear to be of this world."

★★★★★★★★★★★★★

Chapter Two

★★★★★★★

1000.

Captain Abraham "TC" Creighton stood in the turret of his MBT, a state-of-the-art main battle tank; solar-powered, the "Ribald's Chariot," as the vehicle was affectionately known, was the deadliest piece of equipment on the African continent. More deadly, but barely so, than another piece of equipment he was studying. This piece of equipment was human, or so he knew; though he suspected the subject of Sargeant Steve Puhaly's attention doubted there was a shred of humanity in the tough man.

Puhaly, a stocky, barrel-chested gunner for TC's tank, was also the primary drill instructor at what was now called Base Camp One, the massive multinational military complex in what was once northern Morocco.

"You look like a monkey fucking a football!" shouted Puhaly, who was walking ducklike, screaming into the ear of a strange-looking nomad infantry recruit who had recently joined the MNF.

The nomad was crawling, his butt high, using his feet to push him through the sand rather than his elbows and knees to pull him through the sand.

Which made his ass stick up in the air, a problem every infantry recruit had experienced since the days of Hannibal.

The MNF was getting ready to begin the thrust south; a thrust that would require more troops than they had brought from America, or that the European contingencies could provide.

The logical conclusion was to use the nomads, pitiful survivors of the Cataclysm; descendants of Hell.

Puhaly approached Creighton, saluted, then wiped the sweat from his face. Anger registered on his features. "Dammit, TC, these lightbulbs are not my idea of an ideal recruit. Hell! You give them a rifle and they use it like a goddamned club. We'd be better off issuing tree branches than assault rifles."

"Lightbulbs" was the nickname given this particular group of nomads. Every man, woman, and child had white skin, white hair, even their eyes were white. They scared the crap out of Puhaly the first time he saw them in the High Atlas, where the tribe had lived in the mountains like goats.

TC chuckled, then looked down as the hatch opened over the driver's station. Red-haired, green-eyed, Sergeant Fergus Felot's head popped through the hatch. "Quit your bitching, Steve. I remember when you went through Phase 1 training back at DESFOR. You were the most pitiful excuse for a soldier I had ever seen. I made a soldier out of you. If I can do that . . . you can train these lightbulbs."

"You little bastard." Puhaly reached for the smaller driver, who was nearly a midget, which made him ideally suited to drive, since the tank's driver position was the most cramped position in the tank.

The hatch slammed closed and Puhaly threw a fistful of sand at the Chariot.

Puhaly again wiped the sweat from his forehead. He had a distant look in his eyes. TC could see his gunner, like most of the force, was tired of being a drill instructor and wanted to head "downrange" as they called the enemy territory to the south.

"When are we going back into the field, TC? This shit is driving me nuts. And I'm not the only one. Every soldier in this outfit is sick and tired of the routine. Train. Train. Short patrols. More training."

"You heard the colonel. When we're ready. That includes the nomads."

The colonel was the C in C AfriKorps, Commander in Chief, Colonel Thomas Clayton. Clayton had served under TC's father in the early days of the new American military; when the Cataclysm was ending and the specials, those selected to live in the biospheres, had come out to resettle the country and eliminate or rehabilitate the pitiful human remnants who had survived the Cataclysm without the advantages of the specials.

They were called the "hostiles."

A fancier name wasn't necessary.

Climbing down from the turret, TC decided to go for a stroll. The training field was divided into several distinct areas. There was a weapons range for pistols and light automatic weapons. The physical-training area was the most despised, as was the case in most armies. There was even a heavy-weapons range where the recruits learned the use of mortars, heavy machine guns, and rocket launchers.

The stroll was, in many ways, like walking through a battlefield at the height of a raging firefight. But he knew that here, unlike on the battlefield, he was safe. At the far end of the camp he went through a small gate; no fence was connected to the gate, just an arched gate standing like a promontory.

Several rows of small, oblong mounds lay stretched across the desert sand. At the end of each mound was a small headstone marking the grave of an AfriKorps soldier. One particular headstone drew TC like metal is drawn to a magnet.

"Silver Allenbey-Creighton," he read softly. "Captain. Medical Corps. AfriKorps."

They had been married before leaving the Vegas Biosphere. She had been murdered within weeks of their arrival. His eyes travelled to the west, to the solitary stockade area. A ribbon-wire-topped fence surrounded the buildings housing several prisoners. One was named Benhaddou, the murderer of his wife. He had wanted to kill Benhaddou the night he had captured the nomad in the desert. He had chosen to let the man live, knowing his life in a cage would be the worst form of punishment.

"I thought I might find you here," a voice called from behind.

TC turned and saw Colonel Clayton standing in the archway. He was a stocky soldier; his hair dark, but graying at the temples. His brown eyes were framed by deeply tanned skin that was the color of bronze.

The two walked to Clayton's vehicle, a low-profile jeep; a light machine gun sat on a turret atop the vehicle. The windows were hardened glass, capable of deflecting any type of light-weapon projectile.

The drive to headquarters was in silence. TC still blamed Clayton for Silver's death. It was Clayton who had extorted TC's participation in the AfriKorps by drafting Silver to be the medical officer of the unit. Clayton knew TC wouldn't let Silver go to Africa without him.

Finally, TC said what was on every soldier's mind. "We're getting tired of sitting on our duffs, colonel. The troops are starting to rebel."

Clayton knew. Fights were now becoming more commonplace in the billets. Training for the sake of training was causing the men to lose their fighting edge.

"We can't move until we're ready. Operation Iron Necklace depends on having the nomads—as many tribes as possible—under our command. Which means pacified and trained."

Operation Iron Necklace was Clayton's plan; the AfriKorps' OPLAN-3, Operational Plan Three, for the thrust south into enemy territory. AfriKorps was a large, highly trained and equipped unit, the spearhead of the drive south, but not large enough to hold ground once taken. And Clayton was the kind of officer who only paid for real estate once.

The nomads were trained to be inserted as the garrison units in a long extended line of fortresses, like a necklace around a throat. Moving ever southward, the armored units would roll up the enemy, the nomads would control the taken territory.

"I'm sending you downrange to hook up with Reno and the survey team."

TC looked at him strangely. "I thought he was out on the frontier with that train-building fellow. Surveying for your railroad."

Clayton laughed. He knew TC thought the railroad idea was premature. Clayton felt the railroad was essential to the pacification process; more importantly, to resupply as the line of march extended farther south. Farther from the supply depot at Base Camp One. A track bed was already moving east from Base Camp One into the desert, giving the eastern flank of Quadrant One a rapid deployment form of resupply and fighting equipment.

The railroad would provide various supply depots along the line moving south. Equipment would arrive sooner over rail, and in larger amounts.

"He is. There's something new added to the equation. They had contact last night and have recovered a nomad from the Marauders. Damned strange-sounding person according to Falken. He can't leave the survey team, not if there's activity in that area. And I don't want to stop the survey project. We need that track laid as soon as possible."

"Shona?"

The mystical Shona. The nomad travelling with the Pacification Team. A recluse. A friend.

The brother of Benhaddou, the murderer of TC's wife.

★★★★★★★★★★★★★★

Chapter Three

★★★★★★★

OPLAN-1 was the initial plan devised by Clayton. It included organizing an armored expeditionary force in DESFOR, the desert forces of the western United States. Clayton was selected by the president to be C in C (commander in chief), and was provided with as much equipment as he needed, including giving him recruitment carte blanche throughout the U.S. military.

Clayton selected the finest officers and enlisted men in the country. Most were his own DESFOR personnel. Trained in desert warfare, the DESFOR knew desert fighting the way Major Ezekial Forrest knew the mountain-fighting techniques of the western and northwestern mountains of the United States. More importantly, Forrest was a logistical genius.

OPLAN-2 was Forrest's plan: the movement, initial deployment, and long-range supply of AfriKorps forces. Shipment from CONUS, continental U.S., to the coast of Africa was done by ship. Initial deployment was focused on setting up and building a base camp, an operational springboard that would include the European contingency.

Supply of the advancing elements was what Forrest thought to be the challenge. The environment played a major role in his decision to send for a young man he had once met at the Omaha Biosphere. Colt Derider was an engineer who could build a railroad through any kind of environment: desert or mountains. The young man had trains running through his soul.

Forrest knew for OPLAN-3, Operation Iron Necklace, to succeed, the iron necklace would have to be followed closely by the Iron Horse: the old American Indian name for the train that Derider used.

Forrest liked the idea. It brought back some of the past and would be easier than trying to build a highway. Highways could become lost in a matter of hours from a sandstorm. Railroad tracks might be covered, but they would be there and could be easily cleared by a "plowtrain." Trains could carry more equipment as well; trains could be heavily armed with flatbeds mounted with long-range artillery.

And trains scared the living piss out of the nomads! They thought the train was a beast from Hell.

Forrest was a slow-moving, quick-thinking man with ruddy features and eyes that seemed to never quit moving. Tall to the point of being gangly, Clayton often thought of a giraffe when he saw Forrest coming or going.

But the man knew his job. There was yet another problem involving supply that he hadn't overcome. Water had been the first problem. Portable desalinization units had been set up on the coast to supply fresh water while a larger desalinization plant was being built. Pipe had been laid through the desert; water stations, called oases, had sprung up along the route from the Atlantic to Base Camp One.

Water was pouring through at an incredible rate. Huge rubber bladders filled to 20,000-gallon capacity lay buried beneath the sand, artificial underground water tanks. There was so much water that the agronomist Hamp Floris had arranged for some of it to be diverted to his pet project.

Hamp's Orchard sat on the edge of Base Camp One, and when not in his billet or his office, Floris could generally be found walking through the groves of small trees sprinkling Hamp's Orchard.

There were orange trees, peach trees, banana and date palms, even eucalyptus, which Hamp assured everyone would provide a quick-growing fibrous base to the land.

Now, Hamp wanted to go into farming.

Forrest and Clayton sat in the air-conditioned headquarters listening to Hamp's latest dream for the African desert.

"By growing our own food staples, we can provide better, more nutritious food for our troops, and not be hampered by waiting for resupply from CONUS. The CONUS shipments coming by ship can be supplemented with other necessary items, such as equipment essential to the campaign."

Forrest liked the idea. He had a real problem with space available on the ships. The new American Navy only had a few ships, and they were constantly in transit between Philadelphia and the African coast. Growing their own food could save a lot of time, and provide better foodstuffs for the troops.

Clayton laughed. "Now you want us to go into the farming business, Hamp?"

"Yes, sir. I can use nomads as the labor. They're strong, eager, and they learn fast. Besides, in the future, farming will have to be a part of the operational planning." Hamp was grinning at Clayton.

"You sonofabitch, Hamp. Have you been reading over my shoulder?" Clayton asked playfully.

Hamp winked. "It's a small camp, sir."

Clayton, in devising OPLAN-4, had indicated farming would be essential to the downrange areas if food was to be provided on a steady basis. OPLAN-4 was a plan that covered the settlement of an area after it had been defused of hostile activity.

Defusing an area was not done militarily; that was the second option. The first, and most preferred, was to send in pacification teams composed of pacified nomads. The pacification teams, or PT's, or Pac-Teams, would then try to convince the other nomads of the threat from the advancing Marauders, and that the MNF offered protection. And food. Once the nomads agreed to join forces, the general welfare of the tribes was the first consideration.

First on the agenda were medical examinations, followed by clothing and other human needs. Food was high on the priority list since the diet of most nomads was often based on a "whatever crossed the trail" concept. The pot wasn't always filled with enough to provide a proper diet for one, much less dozens or scores of the nomads.

Children had been found in terribly malnourished condition; the adults weren't much better. Knowing an army fights and moves on its stomach, and that an enemy can be controlled through its stomach, food was a powerful weapon.

Travelling with the PT's was a large commissary capable of feeding hundreds of people at one time. Thus far, the PT's had been successful in bringing into the AfriKorps hundreds of nomadic tribes that might otherwise be potential enemies.

Food and the promise of protection were high on the proposal list.

Especially protection. The nomads, having survived the Cataclysm, were now facing the advancing horde from the south called Marauders.

Behind the PT's was the survey unit led by Falken.

Clayton turned to a map of the continent and tapped a spot marking the point where Falken and the survey team had made contact with the Marauders.

"A probing unit, I suspect," said Clayton.

It had been several months since the last field engagement with the Marauders. Reconnaissance units were reporting the Marauders' main line of forward movement was still hundreds of miles south, extending along an easterly line in what was once Algeria.

Forrest studied the area, then commented, "Colonel Forchette is in that area, sir. She's patrolling the outer perimeter with a full squadron. Her squadron may have unknowingly penetrated Marauder lines without knowledge of how deep they've gone."

Clayton gave that possibility some thought. Colonel Marie Forchette, French Army, was his MNF counterpart. She was the point of the spear moving ahead of the PT's and Falken, reconnoitering the area and providing advanced security for the pacification unit. Under her command was an armored squadron of MNF tanks; outdated by comparison to the MBT's of AfriKorps, but more than capable of confronting Marauder armor.

Only Forchette, as the commander, was commanding one of the American-built MBT's with its sophisticated technology and computerized weapons systems.

A perturbed look spread across Clayton's face. Communications were the weak point in the AfriKorps composition. In the years before the Cataclysm, through satellites, communication from one side of the world to the other was as simple as talking across a room. Satellites no longer existed. In the rugged mountainous terrain, line-of-sight commo was their best means. Distance and physical barriers could all but block the signals.

Forchette was too deep for direct communication.

This made Clayton reconsider his orders for the survey team. "I'll send Creighton and three MBT's to link up with Falken. That'll be a formidable element to find Shona and Forchette."

Forrest agreed. "Do you know what area Shona is moving through?"

Clayton pointed at the map. "Sector Twelve."

The map was broken into twenty sectors. Each sector was either the color green, yellow, or red. Green was pacified. Yellow was a positive, ongoing pacification. Red was hostile. Sector Twelve was yellow. The sectors surrounding Sector Twelve were red.

"He's on the cutting edge."

Clayton laughed, replying, "He usually is."

★★★★★★★★★★★★★★

Chapter Four

★★★★★★★

Shona was a tall, black-skinned warrior whose reputation was known throughout the desert. A former chief of the Moroccs, until overthrown by his brother Benhaddou, Shona was a combination of warrior and prophet. To the AfriKorps, he was a means of communicating with the nomads, whose trust was crucial to the success of the operational planning.

His counterpart was Telfi, a lean albino, the product of genetic mutation. Telfi, the chief of the Sharawi, was standing beside Shona on the floor of a desert valley in the southernmost sector.

In the land once called Algeria.

In the distance, a range of mountains formed a horseshoe; what lay beyond the mouth of the horseshoe was a vast desert.

Both men's faces reflected their disgust at what they saw.

Bodies of nomads, a tribe of what Shona called "sand people," those who preferred the openness of the desert to the mountains, lay dead, spread throughout the burning remnants of what had once been their village.

"Marauders." Shona spoke to Telfi in the albino's language and couldn't hide the anger in his voice. He had seen enough destruction to last a lifetime. He could only wonder . . . would it end?

Telfi, the tall white-haired chieftain, walked slowly forward. His chest bore a tangle of scars stretching to his navel. Proud scars. Battle ribbons of a warrior chief. But that was from the past. Before the AfriKorps. He now carried an automatic weapon and wore a pistol on his hip, but in his free hand was the staff symbolizing his Sharawi rank: a spear with a skull mounted on one end.

Some things had to stay as they were.

Behind the two followed a contingent from AfriKorps, a PT complete with three MBT's and two IFV units. A heavy truck transported water, medical supplies, and the commissary. Slowly, the caravan inched its way through the destroyed village.

The smell of burned flesh stung at their nostrils; vultures, one of the few survivors of the Cataclysm, broke from their feeding around several bodies and lifted, shrieking into the air.

Shona pointed. Deep ruts etched the hardened sand. "Tank tracks."

The tracks led out into the desert. The desert was now called the Sahra, but two centuries before it was called the Sahara.

Shona turned as a young tank officer approached. Lieutenant Mike Armbrust was on his first combat tour. Raised in northwestern America, he had transferred to AfriKorps from MounFor. A highly skilled expert in martial arts, his light-brown hair was nearly blond from the sun. His face was richly tanned; his blue eyes flaming from the sight of the dead nomads. Like other American soldiers, he was dressed in desert-camouflaged short-sleeve shirt and shorts, with a drooping hat that protected the neck and face. In his hand he gripped the pistol stock of an automatic rifle with grenade launcher mounted beneath the barrel.

"Let's search for survivors," Armbrust said firmly.

The huts had been easily ground to shreds by the attacking Marauder tanks. In some, beneath the thatch and sticks, and chunks of sand used for the walls, bodies lay crushed. One particular sight was gruesome. The body, whether male or female no one could tell, had been run over from head to foot; usually, a tank crosses a body at an angle.

"Poor bastard." Armbrust pointed at the body's hands and feet. The body had been staked out—spreadeagled—before the tank had made its grisly run. What remained could have been soaked up with a sponge.

Lost in his thoughts, Armbrust studied his map while Shona and Telfi swept the village. After completing his perusil, Armbrust thought he heard a strange sound. He looked up to see Shona approaching. He carried something small in his arms.

The sound of a baby crying floated over the dry land; over the dead.

Shona carried the child with an affection Armbrust had never seen displayed by the desert warrior. Both man and child seemed to glide above the sand toward the "Hummer," a modern jeep with a red cross painted on the front and sides.

A medic took the child and knelt in the shade, laying the baby on a soft nylon blanket. "Doc," as the medic was called, did a quick examination.

"Amazing," said the medic, wiping the sweat from his forehead. "The desert should have sucked the child dry of all bodily fluids."

Doc took the child's finger. There was playfulness in the baby, who couldn't have been more than three months old.

"I'll start an I.V. But we'll have to transport the little

guy to the rear. What he needs is a hospital. And a mother." Doc smiled at Telfi, who seemed to understand.

Checking his watch, Armbrust made a decision. "This sector is swept clean. I don't see any point of continuing further. We're out of radio range inside this valley. From Falken's position we can contact Colonel Clayton and get further instructions." He pointed at the tanks. "If the Marauders are on the move I don't want to get caught this far from our units."

"I suggest you reconsider, lieutenant. The child is indeed important. Important to your mission."

Armbrust didn't understand. "How's that?"

Shona took the baby's left hand and turned up the palm. There was a symbol tatooed onto the palm. The symbol was in the shape of an oval with a dot in the center.

"The mark looks like an eye. What does this mean?" asked Armbrust.

"It is the mark of the Timgad."

"Who in the hell are the Timgad?" Armbrust had come across some strange tribal names since leading the pacification team, but the Timgad was as strange-sounding as it was unfamiliar.

"Nomads. From the desert."

Armbrust shook his head. "We can't go out there. That's not in my orders. But how did the baby wind up here?"

Shona shrugged. "There is only one way to find that answer."

Armbrust again shook his head. "Not without orders."

Shona gripped Armbrust's wrist gently. "The Timgad will be very grateful for returning the child."

Armbrust could see the suggestion reflecting in Shona's eyes. "What direction do the Timgad live?"

"The Timgad live in the desert." He pointed east, toward the openness of the Sahra.

Armbrust looked around. The mountains were too high for radio reception. "You're asking me to violate my orders."

"I'm asking you to return a child to her people. People you will want as allies. Not enemies."

Doc had inserted a needle into the vein of the child's arm and the I.V. now began a slow drip of saline solution. Within minutes the child had settled down and was sleeping on the blanket.

"Doc, can she travel?" asked Armbrust.

"Yes, sir. She's weak, but she can travel."

Armbrust turned to Shona. "Let's move."

★★★★★★★★★★★★★

Chapter Five

★★★★★★★

2000.

Falken heard the steady hum of the solar engine before he saw the low image of Creighton's MBT slip through the electronic minefield surrounding the IFV's night bivouac. One by one, like fast-moving tortoises, the tanks entered Falken's position.

Unbuttoning his hatch, Creighton pulled himself up onto the lip of the cupola and sat there for a moment watching the mechanized infantry commander approach. Both men were friends since childhood; both grinned from ear to ear.

"I understand you ran into some trouble last night," TC commented, watching Reno pull his muscular frame onto the turret of Ribald's Chariot.

Reno settled onto his haunches—his expression seemed to be a "what the hell" smirk—then stuck out his hand, saying somewhat sarcastically, "Good to see you, too, TC."

TC gripped the hand. "What's up?"

Falken laughed. "Damndest creature I've ever seen. Not one of your run-of-the-mill hostiles. Looks like a cross between a lightbulb and a Morocc."

"This fucking place gets stranger by the day." TC checked his watch. "Have you heard from the Pac-Team?"

Falken took a swig of water from his canteen and handed the canteen to TC. "Negative. They are well out of radio range."

"I've been instructed to take your element and the nomad to Shona. Then we find Forchette. Clayton's afraid the Marauders are on the move to the east."

"What makes him think that?"

"The Marauders you tangled with. Why are they in the mountains?"

Before Falken could reply, Puhaly's head popped through the gunner's cupola; his voice was gruff. "If you girls are through holding hands, me and this sawed-off tank jockey would like to come up for air. Fergus hasn't bathed in two weeks. He's getting ripe. I'm getting nauseous."

While the MBT's in TC's squad formed a broader perimeter, the two officers walked to Reno's IFV, which would serve as the command post.

Derider and Roman were sitting on the ground. Between them sat the young girl. She was playing with a miniature train. A model of the type that had been brought to Africa.

"The trainman's going to be pissed off. He wants to build that railroad as fast as possible."

TC looked unconcerned. "Better to be pissed off—than to be pissed on. We'll be back in a few days." He then studied the nomad child. "Has she said anything intelligible?"

"Nothing we can understand. Not in words. But Roman appears to have broken the ice."

Creighton eyed her dress of gold. "She certainly isn't dressed like a nomad."

"She doesn't act like a nomad. She has a certain . . . air about her. As though she were royalty."

Looking at the jeweled crown, TC figured she might

be royalty. "Royalty? But from where? That crown she's wearing must be hundreds of years old, Reno."

Sensing the men were talking about her, the child stood and walked to Creighton. She clasped her hands together and bowed slightly; all the while her red eyes remained on Creighton.

TC felt a shiver streak along his spine as he stared at the eyes; eyes that glowed like banked coals.

"Jesus. She's unnerving."

The child smiled, as though understanding. As though sensing what she expected from the man with bronze skin and brown eyes.

TC motioned her back to Roman. "What do you think it means?"

Falken had been trying to answer that question since the night before. "No idea. She's in good health. Well dressed. Makes me wonder if she might be from . . ." His voice trailed off, but left an impression TC understood.

"Biosphere?"

"She was travelling with Marauders. They're the only people we know of on the continent who were biosphere-protected during the Cataclysm."

"You said *travelling*. I thought she was a prisoner."

"It *appeared* that way. I emphasize the word *appeared*."

"Why do you sound suspicious, Reno?"

Falken's jaw tightened. "Marauders don't generally take prisoners. Even children."

TC started walking off. Falken followed. "Do you think she's a spy?"

"Possible. But what could a child do?"

TC looked at him seriously. "Kill three Marauders with a knife!"

★★★★★★★★★★★★★

Chapter Six

★★★★★★★★

0300.

Major Jan Kaspar knelt behind a dune overlooking the enemy bivouac. The three MBT's were drawn up in a defensive perimeter; two smaller infantry fighting vehicles were dispersed within the main battle tanks. He had sat there for hours, watching the enemy plant mines. Electronic mines that would form a cocoon of safety around the position.

But Kaspar was no fool. He wasn't prepared to attack. Not yet.

Kaspar, the commander of a Marauder probing unit, had conceived a plan that, if successful, would give him what he wanted: an enemy tank to study.

Reports from three months back indicated the Marauders' forward probing units had been destroyed by armored elements that vastly exceeded the technology the Marauders—or rather, ancestors of the Marauders—had uncovered seventy years before when they succeeded in penetrating and capturing the Johannesburg Biosphere. Over the years, the South African Biosphere specials were forced to teach the Marauders the technology until the day came when the specials were no longer useful. The execution of the last special was significant. The Marauder tribe was prepared to exercise the pursuit of their own destiny.

Even Kaspar's name was stolen from the dead. He didn't know his surname. He knew nothing of who his ancestors were at the beginning of the Cataclysm. The specials who had been allowed to live had taught the Marauders the history of the world; the use of science. Military organization and tactics. The importance of power and food to control others. A cruel trick, one once played on the Marauders, had been reversed and now the control was in the hands of those who knew how to use power.

Those who had survived the Cataclysm on the outside.

The combination had allowed the Marauders to sweep up the African continent like modern-day hordes from the days of Genghis Khan. Tribes of nomads had been slaughtered, or turned into slaves. Some had been trained as soldiers, but were not trusted farther than a Marauder could spit.

Kaspar's former commander, Colonel DeBoer, had died trusting the Morocc chief, Benhaddou. The Europeans—as the enemy was called—had the Morocc chief in prison at their northern camp.

Why the Europeans had imprisoned and not killed the Morocc was something Kaspar didn't understand. Nor would he try. Trying to fathom concepts he didn't understand was not a soldier's task; that was for philosophers, and all the philosophers were now dead.

He had to have one of the tanks!

Sliding down the dune, he loped off slowly toward where his troops were bivouacked. If his calculations were correct, he would have his tank by the time the sun reached its zenith!

★★★★★★★★★★★★

Chapter Seven

★★★★★★★

0700.

Lieutenant Armbrust's body ached; his eyes burned and his gut felt as though he had swallowed molten steel. Pulling himself to his feet, he fought through a wave of grogginess the like of which he had never known. Illness was nearly nonexistent since the Cataclysm. What diseases existed outside the biospheres were protected against by inoculation. Or so he thought.

The moment the sun hit his head, he nearly collapsed. Looking around, he saw what he could only imagine in a nightmare: his troops lay sprawled in the sand. They lay motionless, except for a few, and those few were writhing in the sand in obvious agony.

The sound of the baby crying wafted through the heat waves rising from the desert. The brilliance of the sun was such as he had never known before. Just when he thought he would go blind, a figure stood between him and the sun, forming a curtain against the penetrating light.

Armbrust tried to rise, but the searing pain in his stomach drove him back to his knees. Then he felt the impact of something hard against the side of his head and the heat and the sun turned into a cold blackness.

He didn't hear the laughter of Major Jan Kaspar.

Nor the sound of his men's throats being cut as they lay helpless in the sand.

Nor did he feel the sting of a needle entering the vein in the bend of his arm. A sting his men would not be privileged to enjoy, for Kaspar needed only one European to show him how to operate the new-style tank.

★★★★★★★★★★★★★

Chapter Eight

★★★★★★★

1200.

Creighton was in the lead of the column, watching through his field glasses as Falken's IFV reconnoitered the village to the front. The village was smashed; beyond its fallen outline lay the desert. Heavy tank treads streaked east and disappeared into the vastness of the Sahra.

Puhaly's head popped through the cupola. "Jesus. The bastards smashed through those people like they were ants."

The gunner climbed out of the tank and dropped to the hardened ground. The column was stopped where they had the advantage of high ground while Falken conducted the recon. Puhaly took a rock and rolled it through his fingers, watching the IFV as Falken made another search for survivors.

"They won't find anybody alive, TC," Puhaly said flatly. He threw the rock; the skipping sound of the rock echoed softly. "They never leave survivors."

TC spit. Then something caught his attention. Raising his field glasses, he scanned to the east. Several faint objects could be seen drifting over the desert.

"Saddle up, Steve."

"What's happening?"

TC pointed to the east. Puhaly took the binoculars

and watched for several seconds. Lowering the glasses, there was a look of momentary urgency on his face.

That was when Fergus's head popped through the driver's hatch. "What's taking so bloody long, TC?"

"Shut up, Fergus," Puhaly snapped. "We've got scavengers."

"Scavengers? Bloody right we've got scavengers. This whole bloody hellhole of a continent is filled with scavengers."

"Not the two-legged kind, Fergus," TC added. He pointed to the dark spots drifting above the desert.

The driver knew what the spots were: "Buzzards!"

★★★★★★★★★★★★★★

Chapter Nine

★★★★★★★

The column of MBT's streaked across the desert at full speed, taking up an "in-line" form, churning side by side in battle-spread formation. The IFV's were deployed to the flanks, prepared to engage the enemy should they attack from the sides. Derider was in Falken's IFV, and all he could think of was the fact that he was charging across the desert, enclosed and completely blind to what was going on around him. Or why.

Roman said nothing; he had gradually grown accustomed to the suddenness with which things happened in Africa. Besides, he was in the hands of two young officers he had watched grow from rambunctious children to highly motivated fighting men: Creighton and Falken.

The ride in the IFV was not as smooth as in the MBT's. The thick rubber tires of the lighter vehicles didn't absorb punishment the way the tanks were designed to do. The tanks, moving on treads made of special ceramics, could run at full speed and fire their 120mm cannons accurately without slowing for targeting or reloading. The IFV's had to slow down to engage; and feeling the bumpy ride meant the IFV's were moving too fast to engage, which meant they weren't necessarily attacking, nor would they be fired at.

At least, that was the logic of the philosopher, which

allowed him to suppress his distress more readily than the engineer, who was obviously distraught.

The young child sat beside Derider, obviously excited about the whole affair. The hull of the IFV was lined with webbed seats; in the other seats sat infantry soldiers, their weapons poised outward through gunports.

Falken was riding topside, hatch unbuttoned, stationed behind a heavy 30mm armor-piercing "chain gun." The hot air whipped his blond hair back, revealing the thin strip of untanned skin at his hairline. Goggles covered his eyes; eyes that quickly narrowed at something appearing along the slope of a long dune stretching toward his vehicle like an opened hand on the desert floor.

"TC. We have something moving to the front." He squinted, then made out the outline of a human figure. "It's a single target. Appears to be human."

TC shifted to the vision block in his turret. Through the slot he could see the figure walking steadily along the dune; finally, the figure disappeared in a narrow space between two dunes, then reappeared again at the crest of another dune.

TC studied the terrain. The desert was open to the left. The fingers of dunes were to the right. If the enemy armor was in a hull-up position, pulled up tight and hiding behind the dunes with their guns ready to fire at the vulnerable bellies of the AfriKorps tanks as they crossed the dunes, they had chosen the wrong tactic. TC was preparing to flank the dunes.

"All tanks, move to echelon right formation."

In that formation, the tanks would be slotted behind each other, with a staggered separation trailing to the right of the forward tank.

"Tank two . . . follow me into the slot behind the first dune. Tank three and four . . . rotate around the dunes and come in from the back side. Reno, you and your IFV's maintain outer-perimeter security. If anything comes out . . . bust their ass!"

Puhaly loaded a HEAT round into the breech of the 120mm cannon. Gripping the handgrips on the gunner's controls, he waited to activate the laser rangefinder. Close in, as the fighting would be, he would use the rangefinder to lock onto the enemy tank by firing a laser beam at the target. The heat-seeking laser would return backscatter, giving the range and precision aiming needed for an accurate shot, even if his tank was moving at top speed.

Through the vision block, TC saw the figure suddenly raise its arms into the air. His finger was about to fire the main coaxial machine gun when—suddenly—he recognized the man who was waving from atop the sand dune.

"Break off attack. Repeat. Break off attack. Do not fire. Repeat. Do not fire." TC switched the co-ax to the safe position and spoke to Puhaly. "A friend is coming."

Puhaly studied the man through the periscope. "He looks like hell."

Over the commo net, Falken's voice asked, "What in the hell is going on, TC? What do you see?"

TC laughed. Looking at the man walking toward him, Creighton replied, "Shona!"

Then his stomach tightened as he wondered: *Where's the Pac-Team?*

★★★★★★★★★★★★

Chapter Ten

★★★★★★★

"*This will cool* you off, old friend."

Creighton held a bottle of water over Shona's head; a waterfall of the cool liquid splashed from his head to his shoulders, then to his chest, which was stripped bare. Derider sat watching quietly as Roman held the black man's hand, attending the desert warrior as though he were his long lost brother.

The strange-looking child sat off to the side, staring intently at Shona. When their eyes finally met, he seemed perplexed by her presence, as though the sun had bleached away a part of his brain that should allow him to know who she was—or what she was. But he could only stare in bewilderment.

"What happened?" TC asked softly.

Shona began slowly, giving as accurate a report as possible. "We were crossing the desert, toward the land of the Timgad." He pointed toward the east. "We had stopped for the night in bivouac. Late that night, when the moon was at its peak, I heard several groans from the men and went to inspect. What I saw was horrible. The men were writhing on the ground; their bodies burned with fever. Most were delirious, and some began hallucinating. I saw one soldier shoot another soldier he thought was an intruder."

Creighton looked at Roman. "Any thoughts?"

Roman's lips pursed slightly. "I have read of certain forms of disease that can drive men insane."

"Disease?" barked Puhaly. "We're supposed to be immune to all forms of disease."

"Yes. To all *known* forms of disease. Perhaps there is one we are not immune to. A disease that we've never encountered," Standish replied.

"The bastards," Puhaly hissed.

There was something Creighton didn't understand. "How did the disease contact our men? Disease has to be transmitted, it can't just jump up from the sand."

Shona had had many hours in the desert to reach his own conclusion. "The child. The Timgad baby was the source of the disease. I can think of no other way."

"Jesus," TC breathed heavily. "You mean the Marauders—or some other group—set up Armbrust's column by planting an infected baby?"

"Why would they do that, TC?" asked Fergus.

"Fergus—you've got shit for brains," Puhaly snapped. "It should be obvious: they wanted to get their hands on one of our MBT's."

TC couldn't hide his anger. "They couldn't fight us in the open, or capture us in bivouac. They had to find a way to disable the men. They were vulnerable. Damn. What a ruthless bunch of bastards."

"I did not want to leave your men, TC," Shona said without shame in his voice. "I thought it would be better if I tried to escape. To warn you of what happened. I imagine by now your men and equipment are in the hands of the Marauders."

TC understood. "I doubt you could have been of much help." He cursed, "Damn, three MBT's, two IFV's, and more importantly—all those men. The Marauders scored a major coup on us with this move." Then he looked askew at Shona, and asked what the others were wondering: "How is it you were not affected?"

Shona shrugged. "I suppose I'm immune to certain diseases. Since the beginning of the Cataclysm, many diseases have swept through Africa."

"Antibodies," Roman said flatly. "The people of this continent have developed certain immunities to diseases."

"But not us. Or the baby," TC added.

"No," said Standish. "The protection of the biospheres have apparently had at least one drawback. As for the baby, what immunity the child may have inherited could have been overcome by a massive dose of the disease. I expect the child is probably dead by this time."

"What about Telfi?" Puhaly asked, noticing the Sharawi chief was not with Shona. "Was he affected by the disease?"

Shona shook his large head. "No. He has remained behind."

"Is he with our troops?" TC wondered aloud.

"He stayed some distance away. Hiding. Watching. He remained behind while I crossed the desert. We knew the Marauders would come. He will be waiting to give you the information you need."

Shona's mind was beginning to clear with the cooling effect of the water. Again he looked at the young girl. He motioned her to him. Cautiously, the child approached.

"What can you tell us about the girl?" TC asked.

Shona studied her carefully. The eyes were the most disturbing. Red, like blood. He spoke to her in several strange-sounding languages, none of which the others had ever heard before.

She didn't seem to understand a word.

"She's a strange one, Shona," Puhaly said. "Those damned eyes make my skin crawl. And that white hair. She looks like something from an old science-fiction movie."

Shona didn't understand Puhaly's meaning. "She is obviously not a nomad. Her clothing is not the type worn by nomads." He reached for the crown on her head.

The child suddenly stiffened; her hand went instinctively for the crown.

"Easy child," Shona said reassuringly. "I won't hurt you." He lifted the crown from her head and began a close examination.

The crown was made of gold; jewels of various types, diamonds, rubies, sapphires, and emeralds were seated into the gold. Then he turned the crown over and looked inside.

"Ah," he said softly.

TC knelt beside Shona. "What have you found?"

Shona pointed at what appeared to be symbols etched inside the crown.

Roman's curiosity was kindled. He examined the crown's symbols. "Hieroglyphics. An ancient form of cuneiform. The symbols tell a legend."

Shona reached to the sand and began copying the symbols with his finger. When finished, the symbols had been replicated on the desert. There were four figures.

The first was a four-figure number: 2050.

The second was shaped like a triangle.

The third was oblong, like a capsule, with the stick figure of a human inside the capsule.

The fourth resembled a box with a line moving away at a right angle from the upper right corner of the box.

"What the hell does it mean?" Puhaly asked.

Roman sat down, crossed his legs, then began trying to figure out the meaning.

"The first should be obvious. A date, I suspect. The year 2050. The second symbol I'm not certain of, but the third symbol appears to be a human inside of some type of capsule."

"What kind of capsule?" asked TC.

Roman shrugged. "Years before the Cataclysm, there were those who suspected the treachery of the *Prometheus* Project; those who knew they would not be selected to enter the biospheres."

"Self-contained habitats?" TC added. "I remember Silver once talking about the same experiments. But most of that was speculation. They tried the method called 'cryogenics.' "

"What is cryogenics?" Fergus felt foolish as he asked the question.

"Freezing," TC answered. "The body was frozen in a capsule, presumably set with a time delay that would begin the regeneration process at a predetermined date."

Puhaly knelt by the drawings in the sand. "Do you think she was frozen, and then the capsule regenerated her body?"

"Then captured by the Marauders," added Fergus. "It sounds a little weird."

Shona had said nothing. He ran his fingers through the grooves outlining the fourth symbol.

"What about the second symbol, Roman?" TC asked. "What does this mean? A cave? The place where the capsule—or capsules—were placed?"

Before he could answer, Derider suddenly marched forward. He wore the look of a man who seemed possessed. "Not a cave," he blurted.

"What then?" Roman could see the engineer was obviously moved by some sudden realization.

"My great-grandfather's grandfather was an engineer in central America. He helped build the railroad through Panama. I read in one of his journals that he once visited a temple in Mexico. That was the heart of the Aztec empire. The Aztecs were Indians who were conquered by the Spaniards."

"We know that," said TC. "What's your point?"

"In the journal, there were many drawings, one very similar to the one you see here. The triangle-shaped symbol. In the twentieth century, there was a great deal of speculation that those symbols were a historical record by the Aztecs of visitors who had come from a great distance. The same, identical symbols were found in South America, in the Incan empire. And in other places throughout the world."

"Visitors? What kind of visitors?" TC's voice was laced with caution. He was afraid he was beginning to understand what Derider was suggesting.

Derider looked up. "Extraterrestrials, I believe they were called."

"Shit," laughed Fergus. "You mean little green men from outer space?"

Derider pointed at the black-skinned girl. "Not necessarily green. Not necessarily men."

Fergus felt a sudden chill. "Christ. You mean this child is from outer space?"

Derider shook his head. "I don't know if she's from outer space. All I know is that she is damned strange, even for this world."

Shona interrupted. He was still tracing the outline of the fourth symbol. "I have seen this symbol before. Many times before." His voice was nearly shaking.

"Where?" asked Roman.

Shona pointed to the sky. To the northern sky. "At night. In the sky. The stars form this shape."

Roman swallowed hard. He thought for a moment, then said, "Yes. That is the shape of a series of stars. The Big Dipper."

"Do you know what you're saying?" TC asked incredulously.

Roman ran his finger through the groove outlining the disc-shaped symbol. "Yes, I do, lad. It would mean this second symbol, the disc, represents a spacecraft. In its full meaning, the cuneiform says, 'this child came to this world in 2050, sealed in some sort of capsule aboard a spacecraft launched from some star within the Big Dipper.' "

There was no response to his hypothesis. Just the eeriness of the young girl's eyes staring at the symbols in the sand.

Eyes that appeared to understand fully the meaning of the symbols.

★★★★★★★★★★★★

Chapter Eleven

★★★★★★★

1400.

Falken eased his IFV to a halt, popped the cupola, and climbed out. Dropping to the sand, he worked his way toward the top of a series of dunes. Overhead, the sound of flapping wings broke the stillness whenever one of the circling vultures neared the desert floor. Reaching the top, he peered over.

Then he felt his stomach tighten, followed by a hard convulsion. Finally, he vomited.

That was when he felt a hand touch his shoulder. Whirling, and still caught in the throes of the vomiting spasm, he lashed out with his foot, kicking at the figure now framed in the brightness of the sun.

The figure caught Falken's foot, threw his leg to the side, then stepped away from the sun, revealing himself.

"Telfi. You bleached-out sonofabitch!" Falken groaned. Then he smiled. "It's good to see you."

Telfi took Falken's hand and pulled the officer to his feet. Then both men turned and perused the carnage that lay beyond the dunes.

Armbrust's men lay spread throughout the sand. Their clothes and weapons had been stripped away. Their naked bodies were now the main course on nature's menu. Large black vultures picked at the eyes and faces of the dead men. One vulture, as vultures do, had pecked a hole in the soft tissue of one man's stomach. The vulture had stuck its head through the hole and was pulling the soldier's entrails out through it.

Falken had been sent ahead by Creighton to run a recce through the area. Following Shona's tracks had been easy. Easier than what he had found.

Telfi understood a few words of English, and was improving by the day, but most of their conversation was still through the use of hand signals.

"How many tanks in the Marauder group?" Falken asked.

Telfi thought for a moment. He held up three fingers and pointed to the northeast.

"Three tanks moving northeast," Falken said aloud. Then he walked down the dune, firing his weapon in the air, sending a wave of vultures flapping into the sky. Shrieks filled the air; the flutter of wings sounded like cannon fire. The stench was almost beyond what he was able to accept. Covering his mouth with his bandana, he began the gruesome task of the body count.

When finished, he went back to the IFV and got on the radio.

"TC, I've found the bivouac. Or what was a bivouac."

"How many survivors?"

"None. They were all killed."

"What about Armbrust? Did you find his body?"

"Negative. I found the body of a baby. But not Armbrust. He appears to be the only one missing."

"And the equipment?"

"Gone. Nothing here. Somehow they figured out how to get the MBT's fired up and moving." He paused. "We've got to recover those MBT's, TC. Clayton will fry our asses if we come back with this sort of report."

On the other end, Creighton knew Falken was right. What a shitstorm was coming down. He couldn't believe the situation: three MBT's and crews, along with two IFV's, a mobile commissary, and equipment from a Pac-Team captured; sixty men dead and the commander taken captive.

Not to mention the absurd speculation that they were now travelling with a child from outer space.

"Shit," Creighton spit over the radio. "Hold your position. We're *en route.*"

Creighton ordered one of the IFV's to return to Base Camp Silver with a situation report. The rest of the vehicles stormed through the desert, running at full speed toward Falken's position.

To where Creighton's dead soldiers lay butchered.

★★★★★★★★★★★★★★

Chapter Twelve

★★★★★★★

Again the darkness had surrounded Armbrust, who lay with his hands tied behind his back on the sand floor inside a tent. The sounds of men talking could be heard; then boots scuffing through the sand. A voice was barking orders; the voice grew closer, then a man stepped through the flap of the tent.

Kaspar knelt by Armbrust; gripping the American by the hair, he pulled the soldier over until their faces met.

"Your name?" Kaspar demanded.

Armbrust watched as the blond Marauder slipped a dagger from a boot scabbard. "Armbrust. Michael. Lieutenant. AfriKorps. And that's all you get."

Kaspar chuckled. He ran the cutting edge of the blade along Armbrust's cheek. A trickle of blood oozed down to his chin. "We'll see, lieutenant."

He stood and started for the flap. "Your men are dead. Your equipment has been captured. For all practical purposes, you are no longer a military factor. However, you will serve a useful purpose. You will serve—or die. And the death will not be pleasant. That I promise."

When Kaspar was gone, Armbrust rolled over to the sand and rubbed his wound in it. He rubbed harshly, to staunch the flow of blood and fill the cut with the sand, which would serve as a natural bandage.

Then his mind went to work, with the only thoughts he had had since regaining consciousness:

Escape! Revenge!

★★★★★★★★★★★★★

Chapter Thirteen

★★★★★★★

2000.

The sickening task of burying his men had begun with the recurring pain the AfriKorps troops had experienced upon discovering their comrades were dead. All had seen death before; none had seen such numbers of their own dead at one time. The shock they were experiencing was immediately noticeable to Roman, who counseled TC to be cautious.

"You can't run headlong into this situation, lad. You are a soldier. A leader. You have to conduct yourself with professionalism, even though that may be difficult."

TC said nothing. He walked off toward the series of mounds being formed by the burial detail.

Shona sat at the edge of the perimeter with the child, whom he had named Mandi. His oldest daughter had been named Mandi. Try as he did, he was unable to form any sort of dialogue with Mandi. She merely stared at him with those flaming red eyes. Eyes that despite their horrific appearance, made him feel that she was not to be feared.

Could it really be? He wondered. From another planet? The thought was beyond his comprehension. He had seen many strange events in his life. And many strange people who were products of genetic mutation from the Cataclysm. But from another planet?

There had to be another explanation.

Roman joined them and offered Shona one of the field ration kits. Shona ate slowly, then offered food to Mandi.

"She hasn't eaten anything since we found her. Nor has she taken water. It's as though she doesn't require nourishment. Nor sleep. I haven't seen her sleep. She sits there, staring through those bloody red eyes. Quite unsettling, actually."

Three hours later, the desert night was turning cold, as the desert night will. The temperature had dropped thirty degrees in less than an hour. Sentries had been posted; mines placed in the outlying perimeter.

TC and Falken were sitting beside Ribald's Chariot, studying the night sky overhead. The form of a series of stars burned in the darkness. Stars shaped in the form of a dipper.

"Fucking insane," said Falken. "She's a nomad. There is no such thing as a space traveller."

TC laughed. "What makes you think you have all the answers? She could be from another planet as we are from this planet. There's nothing that says we have a lock on the population of the universe."

"Damned eerie. I'll say that. Those eyes. God Almighty!"

"Where else could she have come from?" asked Puhaly.

Creighton shrugged. "We'll leave her with Shona and Roman. If anybody can find out what is happening—it's them!"

Before another word was said, a flare shot straight into the black night. A loud explosion followed as a parachute was expelled. A bright, burning flare lit up the area as the parachute descended. Swinging through the night, the figures of men running to their positions inside the perimeter cast strange shadows across the sand.

TC climbed into the MBT behind Puhaly, who settled into his gunner's chair and turned on the weapons system. A full 360-degree scan began; there was no return on the thermal imager. The glow from the night vision equipment showed nothing.

The alert lasted for thirty minutes. TC checked with each position. Nothing had been sighted.

Returning to his MBT, Creighton ordered Falken, "Take your vehicle and sweep the perimeter. That damned flare didn't go off by itself."

Reno took his IFV and five troops. The minefield was shut down electronically, and once the IFV passed through, the field was reactivated.

TC sat by the radio, listening to Reno, who was reporting at each quadrant of the sweep.

"All clear from Quadrant One through Five. I'm moving onto Six, where the flare was activated."

A long silence followed. Finally, Falken's voice came over the radio. He sounded out of breath. He sounded, TC realized, hearing the sound for the first time in his life from his old friend—frightened!

"You better get out here, TC. I mean now, old buddy. You're not going to believe this. And you better bring that red-eyed little girl."

TC didn't understand. But he knew he couldn't sit on his ass and wait for clarification. "Fire her up, Fergus. I'm going for Shona and the girl."

TC walked the short distance to where Shona and Roman sat with the girl they were calling Mandi.

"Shona, Reno's found something outside the perimeter. He said to bring the child."

Shona looked at the child. He nearly fainted. Sitting

before him was a young girl. Gone was the flame of the red eyes. Gone was the black skin. Gone was the white hair.

The child sitting before him was smiling. She had white skin, blond hair, and the deepest blue eyes he had ever seen!

★★★★★★★★★★★★★

Chapter Fourteen

★★★★★★★

Creighton thought he was losing his mind. What had been the strangest-looking child he had seen in his life had transformed into a replica of someone from his past: Silver Allenbey.

She was beautiful! And for a moment TC was a young lad in the Vegas Biosphere, standing with Silver above the rain forest biome, listening to the soft rainfall. The place where he proposed to his late wife.

Shona and the small entourage slid into an IFV and followed TC's MBT through the perimeter to where they found Reno standing beside his vehicle. He had an automatic rifle cradled in his arms. He didn't seem alarmed; he did appear prepared.

Running to Reno, TC asked, "What's the situation?"

"We've got company," he replied, not looking at TC. His eyes were locked on the figures standing in the light beams of the IFV.

TC looked, then his throat went dry. "Jesus."

Standing in the wash of the light were three people; at least, TC thought they were people. Two were obviously men. One was definitely a woman. A woman TC recognized.

The two men were unrecognizable, but they were familiar. At least he had seen something of the same breed. Only minutes before. Before some strange change had occurred in the girl Mandi.

Two men, their bodies black, hair white, eyes flaming like fire, stood cradling what TC perceived to be weapons from the twenty-first century. They wore clothes that reminded him of pictures he had seen from the twenty-first century.

The third member of the party, a woman, was dressed in the same uniform as Creighton and the others. She wore the shoulder boards of a colonel in the French Army.

Colonel Marie Forchette stepped from the group and saluted Creighton. Her long black hair was tied in a ponytail beneath her desert cap. On her hip she wore a pistol belt and holster.

"Captain Creighton, I'm glad to see the flare we tripped belonged to friends. For a moment, we thought you were Marauders."

The child Mandi broke from Shona's grip and raced toward the two men with Forchette. One of the men rushed forward, swept her into his arms, and hugged her gently. After several moments, he lowered the girl to the sand, then stepped toward TC.

That's when another strange occurrence began:

With the first step, his black skin turned white.

With the second step his hair turned blond.

With the third step his eyes went from blood-red to deep cerulean blue.

His hand was outstretched to TC in friendship.

TC accepted the grip, and breathed, "I'll be a sonofabitch!"

★★★★★★★★★★★★★★

Chapter Fifteen

★★★★★★★

2100.

Puhaly sat straddling the long 120mm cannon of the Chariot, watching the new arrivals who sat around a fire in the center of the camp. Creighton had not fully understood what had happened, and was listening to Forchette give what she thought was a logical answer to the strange metamorphosis they had witnessed.

"It's a possible mutation of the central nervous system. A mutation that precipitates some sort of neural acceleration. I've noticed the changes of these men during periods of stress, or anxiety."

TC thought he might understand. "In other words, like a person who becomes white-haired overnight after experiencing an enormous fright. Or trauma."

"I believe so. Only, in their case, the chromosomes were affected. Which explains why they all look and act alike."

"How did this change occur?" asked Roman. He was obviously enthralled by this new possibility.

Forchette thought she had the answer; an answer that lay in how the two men had survived the Cataclysm. "When we came upon these two men, they were in the desert. At first, they were very hostile. Hostile to the point that we had to sedate them. That was when we noticed the first change."

"While they were asleep?" asked Creighton.

"Yes."

Roman thought for a moment; one of the child's peculiarities was suddenly making sense. "I never saw Mandi sleep. Not for a moment."

Forchette continued with her theory. "She stayed awake out of fear. But, when they woke up, they immediately reverted to the opposite state. Dark skin. White hair. Red eyes."

"Where do they come from? I have never heard of these people; nor Telfi. I don't believe they are nomads," said Shona as he looked at Telfi, who nodded in agreement.

She had no answer. "I can only speculate."

"What are your thoughts?" asked Creighton. He was watching the two adults, still amazed at what he had witnessed earlier.

Forchette stretched out a map on the sand. Mapping was another victim of the Cataclysm. All mapping was now done on the spot, with the map limited in detail to the area already controlled by the MNF. What new additions there were to the map were provided by Forchette during the reconnaissance mission. Most prominent was a red line moving to the southeast, then turning north along the outer edge of the controlled sectors denoting the route of her reconnaissance mission. She touched a point on the map. "We found these two here."

The spot was in the open desert east and north of their present position. Running her finger due west, she touched the point where Falken and the survey team had encountered the Marauders with the child. "It should be apparent my two were trying to follow the Marauders who had somehow captured the child. The Marauders were moving faster, on vehicles, which was why they outran the pursuers. If that's the case"—

she paused, running her finger again to the east—"I suspect they all came from this area."

The area depicted on the map was empty. Forchette looked at Shona. "Is there something out there?"

Shona shook his head slowly, as though in thought. She looked at Telfi, who shrugged.

Creighton then added to the mystery by explaining the symbols they found on the inside of the child's crown.

Forchette nearly laughed. All the soldiers were grinning embarrassingly.

"I know it sounds crazy," said Creighton.

"Crazy! *Bizarre* is a better word." Forchette turned to the girl, who was sitting quietly between the two men who had pursued her captors.

"Which, in any case, brings us to the question: what are we to do about them?" asked Creighton. "I don't want to force them to accompany our movement. At the same time, I'd like to know what's out there. It could be important in the future. Especially if there are Marauders working to the east. And there must be. Otherwise, why would the group that ambushed Armbrust have moved east?"

"Are you tracking them?" asked Forchette.

Creighton nodded. "Falken is on the trail. He's laying back, being very cautious. We want to recover the MBT's intact. If possible. Otherwise, we will detonate the tanks for security reasons. We can't have the Marauders duplicating the technology on the MBT's." There was something in his voice suggesting the destruction of the tanks was not an unplanned possibility.

"Can you destroy the tanks?"

Creighton grinned. "With the flick of a switch. Colonel Clayton had each of our MBT's rigged with a detonation device that can be activated electronically. The tank commanders are familiar with the procedure. Armbrust will know we're on his trail. He'll be anticipating what will happen."

"Can you save him?" she asked.

TC shook his head. "I don't know. But that's the least of our concerns. The tanks are uppermost on the priority list. The tanks . . . and whatever the Marauders are doing to the east."

Forchette looked off to the east. There was a suspicious look on her face. "Something's going on out there. I don't know what. The Marauders have changed their tactics. I think further investigation is necessary."

TC agreed. "With your permission, I'd like to suggest a plan," TC said.

"Proceed."

He squatted next to the map. "We send Derider with two IFV's and one MBT to the rear and make contact with Clayton. He'll want to know the situation. The remainder of the element will break off into two columns. The first column will close on the Marauders with our MBT's and Armbrust. The second will push to the northeast. To set up a blocking position. If the Marauders are planning a flanking movement, I would rather fight them in the open then in the mountains."

"You think they might be trying to outflank us?"

"I do. It's what I would do if in their position. They know we're patrolling to the west of this position. They know they're outgunned and are ill-equipped for an open-field fight. It's my guess they planned to capture several of our tanks, learn their operation, then use them as a spearhead to hit us on the northeast flank. That's where most of the European elements of the MNF are deployed. Your equipment and theirs is comparable. With our tanks, they could gain an advantage over your MNF forces."

"If what you're suggesting is true, they do have something to the east. Something we hadn't anticipated."

TC nodded. "One helluva big staging area." He glanced at the young girl and her two protectors. "And I'll bet wherever these three came from will put us close to their location."

"Why do you say that?"

"If Shona and Telfi had not heard of these people before now, it must mean they did not *want* to be discovered. The child must have escaped, been captured near Falken, and was being returned to wherever in hell she came from when Falken encountered the Marauders."

"What about the other two? They were armed when we found them. The Marauders wouldn't have allowed them to keep their weapons unless they had joined forces with the Marauders."

Creighton thought for a moment. "There's one other possibility."

"What's that?"

"The child and the two men were *sent* to the west."

She thought about that possibility. "You mean sent to find our forces?"

"That's very possible. A child in a group would suggest non-hostile intentions. But she can be dangerous. She killed three Marauders in the one tank. But to us she has shown no acts of violence since being in our care. The two you picked up have not been hostile. I think they were dispatched to find us. Somehow the girl became separated from the other two, and was found by the Marauders. The three tanks Falken destroyed were probably a probing unit that stumbled onto the girl. Her two tribesmen continued to try and find her. They found you and must have realized you were the people they were looking for."

"What do we do?"

Creighton turned and looked at the three strange people from the desert. He started to say something when the man sitting closest to Mandi stood and approached.

He stood there for a long moment, studying the faces of the AfriKorps personnel. Finally, he raised his arm and pointed to the the east.

Then he spoke the first words any of them had heard from the three strange-looking humans. His English was perfect.

"Your enemies have assembled in the land of the Magi!"

PART TWO
THE CATACOMBS

★★★★★★★★★★★★★

Chapter Sixteen

★★★★★★★

0200.

Reno Falken crept along the edge of a dune, staying in the shadows, pausing to listen for the scuff of feet; the shout of a sentry. The crack of a rifle. The signal that his presence had been discovered.

There was no sound, except the faint whisper of the wind rolling slightly from the east, carrying the smell that Falken had learned to recognize as Marauder. He carefully made his way along the dune, then crawled through the narrow opening where the dune ended and one nearby began. The pace was slowed by his need to continually check for sound; then he would continue. The sweat beaded on his forehead, cascading down his face onto his throat, where his already soaked bandana absorbed more.

He was mentally mapping the Marauder position, noting the outlying listening posts; behind the LP's, the staggered gun emplacements held four soldiers each. Farther to the rear were the heavier armored units. In the center was what appeared to be a command post where the three American MBT's were parked.

That was when he heard the screams of Armbrust, a man he had known since the formation of AfriKorps. The screams were painful to hear; yet, encouraging to the mind of a soldier:

Armbrust was resisting!

★★★★★★★★★★★★★

Chapter Seventeen

★★★★★★★

Years of martial arts discipline had allowed Lieutenant Michael Armbrust to reduce his thought processes to a sharp focus that narrowed his perception to a thin, straight line. Pain, he had learned long ago, could be one of two things: an enemy, or an ally.

Tonight, he concentrated on using the pain as an ally. He knew the torture was designed to break, but not destroy. Were he destroyed, he would be of no value and the exercise of his persecutors would be fruitless. He knew the sole purpose in what he was attempting: his persecutors had to achieve.

He had only to survive.

To survive meant to resist. To resist meant to withstand the brutality; not thinking of the punishment in terms of pain; rather, in terms of reprieve.

Each passing second that he resisted was another second that he denied what was happening to him. So long as he resisted, he would survive. The persecutors couldn't risk killing him, nor rendering him mentally incapable. Which meant he was important.

He had only to survive!

He knew the cavalry was on the way!

"You're a very stubborn man," said Kaspar. He was holding a fire-red piece of metal gripped by a pair of tongs. The metal had been applied without mercy to various parts of Armbrust's skin over the last hour. Result: nothing.

"I'm reaching the limits of my patience, lieutenant. You have two choices: cooperate, or die."

Armbrust forced a grin through a mask of hatred. "Then you have only one choice: kill me . . . if you dare!"

Kaspar's eyes widened. Then a thought came to mind. He said nothing. Rather, he leaned forward with the tong, placing the fiery metal near the right eye of Armbrust.

"Kill you? That would be foolish. I have something else in mind." He held the fiery metal close to the eyeball, watching the light reflect from the iris. Then, there was the searing as the vitreous humor began to shrivel as the metal destroyed the eyeball.

Armbrust was being held upright, his legs and hands bound behind his back. A long rod ran between the ropes joining his hands and feet. At Kaspar's gesture, the four men controlling the tank commander forced his body forward, then jerked upward at the two ends of the rod. Suspended off the floor of the tent, Armbrust's head hung weakly. A sickening stream of mucus drained from the socket where his scorched eyeball was now swimming in a sea of darkness.

When his body went limp, Kaspar raised Armbrust by the hair. He could see it was no use interrogating further.

"Leave him," Kaspar ordered.

The young officer's body was dropped to the sand. Moments later, when all were gone, the muscles in Armbrust's face twitched slightly.

A thin smile cracked his mouth.

The discipline of the soldier took command. In his mind he was on his feet, standing with his knees bent, his fists raised, a karate fighting stance. He pretended he was blindfolded. He listened for the sounds of the attackers. He heard something, then stepped forward, blocking the punch. A kick fired out. He backpedaled, resumed a fighting stance. He was ready for the next attack.

In his mind . . . he was ready! He repeated the scenario over and over.

Fuck the Marauders . . . he was ready!

★★★★★★★★★★★★

Chapter Eighteen

★★★★★★★

"*We came to* this land in the final days before the great Cataclysm. Most of our people were to be part of the forsaken. Those left to the fury of the earth's wrath. Cataclysm! We were scientists, teachers, and some were soldiers. Men, women, and children the governments of the earth had rejected. Rejected. Perhaps there was no choice. We could only speculate since we did not know all the facts. However, there was one fact: not all were selected to be part of the chosen. Most of us were to be left to the fury."

The man talking was the tall Magi who had shown such affection towards Mandi. His skin and features would change with his emotions; from white skin to black, red eyes to blue. Then revert to the previous state.

It was enthralling.

"My name is Carl Eliason. Dr. Carl Eliason. I lived in the state that was called New Mexico. Near Taos."

Roman Standish couldn't conceal the sudden gasp that exploded from his lungs.

"Carl Eliason? Professor Carl Eliason? Of the New Mexico University Center of Advanced Human Studies?"

Eliason smiled slightly, nodding as he spoke. "That's correct. Perhaps you're familiar with my work."

"Familiar? Of course I'm familiar with your work. Your methods were one of the first alternatives considered when the Cataclysm appeared inevitable."

"Cryogenics," Creighton said flatly. "I remember studying you—and your research—in school. You claimed to have perfected the ultimate form of body preservation."

"Not 'claimed.' I did perfect the science."

Creighton looked at the scientist's skin, which was now turning dark. "Apparently not perfection, doctor. There seems to have been a few flaws."

Eliason laughed. Finally, he conceded, "A few."

"Please, Dr. Eliason. Continue with what happened. How you arrived here in Africa."

"The choice of Africa was based on sound judgment. We assumed the effects of the Cataclysm would be devastating, that the world would devour itself during the period it took for earth to reclaim itself. We selected an area of the world we thought would be uninhabited through that time period. An area where we would not be disturbed. The Sahara Desert was already the most uninhabited place on earth, other than the two poles."

"Disturbed by people?" asked Forchette.

"Precisely. People were our greatest threat. Had we been discovered during those years, we would have been at the mercy of God knows what. Or whom."

Creighton was fascinated. "What did you do, Dr. Eliason? How did you survive?"

Eliason sat in the sand. He slowly unfolded the tale while holding Mandi in his lap.

"In the year 2045, there was no doubt to those of us at the Center that the Cataclysm was approaching. I went to Washington and met with the government. The government treated me with disdain. They said there would be no Cataclysm, that it was the theory of hysterical scientists."

"But you didn't believe them?" asked Roman.

"I was a scientist. Myself and others knew the truth. We could interpret meteorological data. All the data indicated the polar regions were already melting at a high rate. It was only a matter of time. And we saw through the ridiculous treaties forged by the major powers. Disarmament. That was hogwash. We knew what it meant. The earth was going to die, and a few were going to survive. A select few. Weapons were destroyed to protect the survivors from those they had betrayed—not to achieve peace!"

His voice was nearly a howl; standing on his feet, holding the child to the darkness of the stars, his eyes turned fireball red.

Puhaly's hand went to the pistol in his holster, but he relaxed the grip as he saw Eliason's appearance change again.

"That's one scary sonofabitch!" Puhaly whispered to Creighton.

"Then you knew of the biospheres?" asked Roman.

"Knew of the biospheres? Of course. Many of our people helped refine the biospheres from the original Arizona Concept."

All those present, with the exception of Shona and Telfi, knew what was meant by the Arizona Concept. The original biospheres had first been designed in the late 1980s and early 1990s, in Arizona, as an answer to survival on a proposed Mars expedition.

"In what way?" asked Creighton.

"Autonomy. Absolute autonomy from the earth itself. The original concept was designed to provide the habitat requirements for a few people. Not hundreds. The resources would have gradually expired through pressure. There wouldn't have been enough continual resources to accommodate such a vast number of inhabitants."

Creighton thought he understood. "The underground water supply sources."

Eliason smiled. "That's correct. The man-made aquifers that lay beneath each biosphere. A great reservoir of water. Water for the biomes, if managed properly, could last for centuries."

TC Creighton thought of the rain forest biome at the Vegas Biosphere. He knew the water was literally created in an environmental duplication of the earth's water production system, but all the inhabitants knew there was water beneath the ground. Water stored, and used over the years, carefully gauged in its annual use to prevent a drought. Gauged to last at least fifty years beyond the projected cessation of the Cataclysm.

"There's something that puzzles me, Dr. Eliason." Forchette was talking. She looked at him with a mixture of suspicion and contempt. "Why weren't you selected for the biospheres?"

"I was selected."

"You refused?"

He nodded furiously. "I offered an alternative. One that could have saved hundreds of thousands. Instead, the selfish few were saved. I wanted no part of that. Besides, I didn't want to live in a capsule, watching the earth die, never knowing if this planet would regenerate. I wanted to live as an inhabitant—or not at all. It was a decision we all made."

"Cryogenics?" asked Roman.

"Cryogenics. Hundreds of capsules were designed for each member of our . . ." He paused, then grinned. "Shall we say . . . 'faction.' "

"You call yourself the Magi," noted Forchette.

"Yes. Magi. The wise men. A rather symbolic gesture, I thought. Wise enough not to suffer a slow death in the biospheres. Wisdom we would share with the future. If there was a future."

"Then I take it you didn't place much confidence in the select—as you call them—surviving in the biospheres?" Forchette asked the question with a certain indignation.

"Not much, to be frank with you. I had no idea any had, until those mongrels invaded our territory last week. They captured a group of our children. We tracked them as far as we could. To a point where the tracks of their tanks split into another direction. I followed the tracks of the smaller group. That was where I was discovered by Colonel Forchette. A group of my people continued to follow the other tracks. I don't know what happened to them. Whether they're alive or dead. I don't even know who the bastards are. All I could do was follow. Follow and hope that I could catch up to them. I didn't know my daughter was alive until I arrived here. She must have managed to escape and was recaptured. I presume they were on the way back to the main element when they ran into your patrol."

"Why would the Marauders waste their time chasing after one little girl?" asked Puhaly.

Eliason shrugged. "She had seen their force and knew the direction of march. We didn't know of your presence, but they did. I suspect they feared what she might divulge had she been found by your people."

"Why doesn't she talk?" asked Roman.

"She's been instructed not to talk to anyone except her own people. And I imagine she was too frightened to talk after what happened."

That was where Creighton took over with the interrogatories. "Those 'mongrels' are from the southern tip of Africa. We know little about them. Perhaps you've learned something of value."

"They are descendants of the 'outsiders,' as they call themselves. They managed to overpower a biosphere and force the inhabitants to teach them everything. Language. Technology. Everything there was available. I presume the original inhabitants were then slaughtered when they outlived their usefulness. What I didn't know about was you. I wasn't aware there was an American presence on this continent."

"There is now," said Puhaly. "We're the AfriKorps."

"AfriKorps? Indeed. What is AfriKorps?"

"A multinational military force sent to this continent to restore law and order. Society. Civilization. Whatever in hell you want to call it. We are trying to stop the northern advance of the Marauders. They seem to have their eyes on the farmland of Europe."

Eliason shook his head in wonder. "Sounds like another man with similar designs on Europe. He, too, had an army in Africa. All this time and the world has learned nothing. Through all this Hell, and the same sort of mindless slaughter continues."

"I noticed you were carrying a gun," Puhaly pointed out. "So don't be so high and mighty."

Eliason laughed. "You're quite correct. We did cache a sizeable arsenal. We weren't certain what we would find when the time came."

"Speaking of which," said Creighton. "Where did you come from. Here in the desert? Where are your people? What was your plan? Did it work?"

"We selected a place we thought would not be of much value once the Cataclysm began. With great difficulty, we brought our people, equipment, and scientific knowledge to an area to the east. We built what we laughingly called the 'catacombs,' the place where the chambers were stored. It was no easy task, I assure you."

"I'm certain," Creighton replied wryly.

Eliason continued, ignoring the quip. "The catacombs was a vault built deep in the earth. Each of our members was installed in a capsule, then processed."

"You mean frozen?" asked Puhaly.

"Precisely. Frozen."

"How were you monitored?" asked Forchette.

"By people called Sentinels. They were programmed to awaken at intervals, make systems checks, and ensure the continued operation."

A new voice was added to the conversation. "We thought you came from outer space," said Fergus Felot.

"What a preposterous notion," Eliason countered.

Creighton pointed to the girl. "The crown she's wearing has a series of symbols. We thought, in light of her appearance, and a loose interpretation of the symbols, that you might be from another planet."

"In a sense . . . we are. Originals from earth before the Cataclysm. The crown is more than two thousand years old. My wife was an archeologist. She dressed our daughter in a gown similar to one she discovered on a mummy in a pyramid on the Nile in 2035. The crown was on the mummy. The mummy was a child. She thought it rather appropriate. The only change my wife made on the crown was to inscribe the year my daughter and us went into the catacombs."

"Where is your wife?" asked Forchette.

A great sadness came over Eliason. He spoke softly. "Not all the chambers worked accurately. We had a 40 percent loss rate."

There was another question Creighton needed answered. "And the change in your physical appearance? What caused that little quirk to develop?"

Eliason looked at Forchette. "You were correct in your estimation. During the processing the constant freezing must have had some effect on the central nervous system. We noticed it right away."

"I'll bet you did," said Puhaly.

"I have one other question," said Creighton. "What about the Marauders? How do you know so much about them?" asked Creighton.

"While looking for my daughter we encountered a small group. Their vehicle had become disabled. We overpowered them and conducted an interrogation."

"Where are they now?" asked Puhaly.

"They were released."

"That was foolish," said Creighton. "You should have killed them."

"We aren't barbarians, Captain Creighton."

"Nor are we. We're soldiers. You still should have killed them." There was no apology in TC's words.

"Fucking-A straight," said Puhaly. "They would have killed you."

The questions continued. The answers were given. Finally, Eliason asked what he had to know.

"The Cataclysm. Was it as bad as predicted?"

Creighton looked at him severely. "It was worse than predicted. It was a living Hell. Inside . . . and outside."

★★★★★★★★★★★★★★

Chapter Nineteen

★★★★★★★

0800.

Creighton and Forchette were conducting a briefing when the steady hum of an approaching IFV warned of Falken's return to the bivouac. Climbing out of the vehicle, Falken was visibly tired. He went straight to a portable shower stall erected near the command post and walked into the cubicle, turning on the water while still wearing his uniform and webbed gear.

"Take ten minutes. Then we'll continue," Creighton ordered the score of tank and IFV commanders gathered for the briefing. He went to the cubicle and leaned through the curtain. Falken was sitting on the floor, water cascading into his lap.

Falken had a distant look, like a man who had something he wanted to say but couldn't find the words. Or the energy to speak.

"Remember when we were kids, TC? We would sneak out of the biosphere and go into the mountains. 'Our own little adventure,' you used to call it."

Creighton remembered. "I know we got our butts in a sling the first time we were caught. The biosphere disciplinary committee treated us like we were criminals."

"Remember that night a group of hostiles camped in the rocks near where we had our camp?"

Creighton's eyes narrowed. "How could I forget? It was the worst night of my life."

"Yeah. The worst night. You still remember, don't you?"

"I do. The screams are with me forever."

Neither said anything. Their minds flashed back to their teenage years, and the night they were hiding while playing a very dangerous game. Each recalled what they saw happen in the hostile camp.

"They cut that poor bastard into little strips, then ate him raw. Blood raw."

TC's facial muscles tightened. He remembered the man, a raggedy, pathetic-looking creature the hostiles had dragged to the center of their camp and began dismembering. Each member removed became a choice morsel to be fought over among the hostiles. It was during the chaos they were able to slip through the shadows and reach the openness of the desert where they were picked up by a patrol the next morning.

"What made you think of that?" asked Creighton.

Falken tilted his head back. The water splashed off his tanned face. Then his blue eyes widened, and he replied, "I had to listen to the same screams last night."

Creighton looked as though he could kill. "Armbrust?"

Falken pulled himself to his feet. "He's resisting. That's one tough sonofabitch."

"By that, you mean he hasn't shown the Marauders how to operate the MBT's?"

"He has not."

A sudden sound in the distance caught TC's attention. He stepped away from the shower stall and looked off to the south. What he saw gave him an idea.

"The Marauders will be on the move. We're going in pursuit. It's my intention to destroy the MBT's if we can't recover them intact."

Falken had already figured that out. "That'll mean the end of Armbrust."

TC grinned. "Not necessarily."

Falken looked at him quizzically. "What do you have in mind?"

Creighton pointed to the southeast. A gray haze stretched across the horizon.

"We'll need Shona and Telfi." Creighton then explained his plan. When he had finished, Falken looked at him incredulously.

"It'll be risky," said the IFV commander.

"We're in the business of risk."

★★★★★★★★★★★★★★

Chapter Twenty

★★★★★★★

1200.

The armor of the Marauder tanks was of the early twenty-first-century design; primarily the West German Leopard, a good tank for its day, but highly susceptible to the elements. Sand, especially, could create havoc on the operation of both the engine and the weapons optical systems.

Bluntly stated, operation inside a sandstorm made the tank all but nonoperational.

And a sandstorm was now raging around the Marauder column Kaspar was leading toward the staging area to the east.

"Damn," he cursed. Through the periscope he could see nothing but the curtain of haze obscuring his vision. His frustration was mounting as every conceivable thing that could go wrong was obviously happening. Armbrust was proving more durable than he had anticipated. Without the American showing him how the tank operated there would be less chance of success when his forces attacked the northeast flank of the European forces.

Fuel was becoming a major concern, since his tanks operated on petrol, as compared to the solar energy that powered the American MBT's. During the march north, major fuel depots had been established along the line; but now, off the route of march of the main element, there was the risk of not having enough fuel. There were fuel reserves to the north, in the European territory, but without the captured American tanks that might be an impossible objective.

He had to learn how to operate the tanks' weapons systems! Their scientists could duplicate the tanks in time; however, he couldn't outfight the enemy with what he was driving, and he couldn't fight with a weapon he couldn't operate.

And time was of the essence. The Americans and Europeans had not pushed south; not yet. That would come soon, and with the new tanks the push would drive the Marauders back. By reproducing the American tanks the future battles could be fought on more even ground. Otherwise, when the Americans began the push south, the Marauders would be fighting a delaying action all the way to the Johannesburg Biosphere.

Which brought him back to his original problem: how to force the American to cooperate.

Looking again through the periscope, Kaspar could see nothing through the blinding sandstorm.

Sirocco!

That's what the sandstorms were called in North Africa. He had seen others in the south, but nothing with this intensity. Procedure demanded that the column halt and wait out the storm. That was fine in the south, where there was nothing to fear. Here, he suspected the Americans would discover the loss of their tanks, then pursue to recover.

He had to reach the staging area.

But first he had to consider the storm. Taking the microphone, he spoke angrily into the commo net.

"All units . . . halt! Form a defensive perimeter around my unit."

Through the haze he could see the tanks slowly enveloping his Leopard in a protective circle.

"Now . . . we wait," he whispered throatily.

★★★★★★★★★★★★★

Chapter Twenty-one

★★★★★★★

1400.

Inside Falken's IFV, a round tracking screen was giving off a steady flash of blue light in the form of a line from a target downrange. The receiver in the IFV indicated the signal was still being received from a transmitter. Locked onto the transmitter with a special receiver, the American forces could locate and plot the location of any of their units that might be lost or disabled in the desert. Even captured. The operator would then set up a heading and the process of tracking onto the target was simple.

The operator turned and called out, "I estimate the target at about 200 meters, Reno."

In the rear, Falken handed Shona and Telfi a pair of goggles; the men slipped the goggles over their faces and adjusted the straps. He then handed them a headset which they slipped onto their ears.

"I can guide you in any direction I need you to go. From what Shona reported yesterday, and from what I saw earlier this morning, Armbrust is being transported in one of the Marauders' IFV's. They are similar to our IFV's. They carry a crew of three, and eight infantrymen."

"How can you tell which one Armbrust is in?" asked Shona.

Falken held up his hand. Around his wrist was an identification bracelet. "There's a small transmitter inside the bracelet. In order for the transmitter to remain dormant, the bearer must reset the automatic activation switch every twelve hours. If, after twelve hours, the activation switch is not reset, a signal begins transmitting. Armbrust knew to not reset his activation switch in the event we were in pursuit. We've picked up the signal and can guide you to the IFV where he's being held. The headset will give us communication, and it will give us your location so we can steer you through the storm, right to their rear ramp."

Shona explained to Telfi in his language. The nomad chief looked genuinely impressed.

They said nothing; both moved to the rear where the ramp was opened momentarily to allow them to slip from the red-light glow inside the IFV to the haze of the storm.

Suddenly, they disappeared.

Shona and Telfi slithered through the sand like two desert snakes, pausing for Shona to receive course instructions. A hail of gritty sand pelted their bodies, which were heavily clothed except at their ears and the exposed skin around the edge of the goggles. Their mouths were clamped tight; each man gripped an automatic rifle with a sound suppressor attached to the muzzle.

Why the silencer? Shona had wondered. In this storm, a cannon would go unheard. But he did as instructed. Perhaps it was part of what they called procedure. The Americans were strong on procedure. So far, it seemed to be working.

Neither man was certain the plan would work until the gray outline of a tank came into view. Telfi pointed at the Leopard sitting wrapped in a fence of sand.

Through the glass plates of the goggles Shona could see the albino's white eyes glow and he knew what the Sharawi chief was thinking. Shona shook his head. They had come for Armbrust, not to destroy Marauder tanks.

Another command came over the radio headset. Shona shifted slightly, adjusting his course. As he passed the rear of the Leopard he knew he was now in the center of the Marauder position.

Another Leopard sat at the center. *The Marauder chief,* he told himself. And a terribly exciting thought shot through his mind. Then he switched to thoughts of why he was in the center of the enemy bivouac.

Falken's voice steered them to their right.

There, in the haze, sat an IFV vehicle. The two slipped to the rear of the IFV and climbed onto the turret. A quick check of the hatch revealed what both had hoped: unlocked.

From his pistol belt Telfi removed a small stun grenade. He pulled the pin and dropped the stun grenade through the hatch. He quickly slammed the hatch shut.

A muffled roar trembled along the top of the IFV, followed by Telfi opening the hatch.

Inside, five Marauder soldiers sat frozen, their brains paralyzed by the flash from the stun grenade. Armbrust was on the floor, lying face down, stunned as well.

Shona and Telfi, wearing the goggles, were protected from the stunning effect of the grenade's chemical, which paralyzes the brain through the optic nerves.

With complete ruthlessness, both men fired their weapons into the bodies of the Marauders. A layer of smoke wafted into the upper recesses of the IFV. There were several cries as the bullets tore through the enemy.

Then silence.

Shona took a syringe and rammed the needle into Armbrust's shoulder. His body was wracked with deep welts. His face was a mass of bruises; one eye was closed.

The injection quickly washed away the stun effect and Armbrust was on his feet.

"We have to hurry," Shona said while checking his watch. "The storm will pass soon."

Helping Armbrust through the turret was the most difficult part of the rescue. Slowly, they made their way toward the outer perimeter. Pausing beside the tank in the center, Shona pointed for Telfi to continue. Over the roar of the wind and the biting sand, the albino heard the black chieftain say, "I will be close behind you."

Telfi watched Shona remove another stun grenade, and as the desert warrior disappeared through the curtain of sand, he knew he didn't have to ask where he was going.

Shona crept along the side of the Leopard, then deftly climbed onto the turret. He unlocked the turret, pulled the pin on the grenade, then dropped the explosive through the hatch.

Again the muffled tremor. Dropping through the turret, he found himself staring into the frozen eyes of a man he had seen only once. A man who had overseen the brutal capture and execution of helpless soldiers.

Shona's hand flashed up; he was gripping a knife. There was the crisp sound of flesh and cartilage being severed with a single cut of the knife.

Kaspar's eyes were filled with horror.

★★★★★★★★★★★★★★

Chapter Twenty-two

★★★★★★★

1330.

The moment the sandstorm passed through the desert, a silence followed. Eerie. Unnerving. The sky was suddenly blue. The sun burned white and there was no sign of movement; not a sound in the Marauder perimeter.

Five hundred yards away there was a sound. A single voice from inside Ribald's Chariot ordering, "Fire!"

Four MBT's stood on line; their guns roared simultaneously.

In the next instance four SABOT rounds streaked from the 120mm smooth-bore cannons of AfriKorps.

The SABOT is the ultimate armor-piercing round; assembled around a "bolt" manufactured of depleted uranium, the SABOT discards upon firing, sending the bolt through the armor of the target. Once penetration is made, the interior of the target tank turns into a hailstorm of flying metal shards.

Escape is impossible. Death is certain, and painful.

A split second after the MBT's fired their cannons, the Marauder tanks turned to burning hulks as the magazines ignited, then the fuel tanks. Creighton suspected none of the Marauders knew what hit them.

With target acquisition computerized, Puhaly had only to sit and watch as the computer automatically reloaded the cannon and turned to the next target laser-locked by the multi-targeting capability of the Chariot.

The Marauder perimeter turned to a burning ring of molten steel; there were no screams. A few turrets flew through the air, landing upside down alongside the occasional human body parts discarded during the explosions of the Leopards.

"Not bad," said Creighton. Through the vision block he counted over a dozen dead Leopards. The three American MBT's and the commissary halftrack sat untouched.

Creighton pressed the switch on his boom mike. "Reno, take your people in and search for survivors. On the way past my position you can drop off our guest." He paused a moment, then ordered, "Send up the MTV."

Climbing out of the tank, Creighton dropped to the warm sand. The MBT's sat in front of other rows of tanks, including the tanks from Forchette's squadron. Through this formation weaved Falken's IFV; following close behind was an MTV, a medical transport vehicle.

Both vehicles stopped alongside the Chariot. Creighton went to the rear of the MTV, opened the door, and looked inside. Lieutenant Armbrust lay on his back on a stretcher; an I.V. tube ran from his arm to the plastic bag suspended from an I.V. pole. His face was bandaged on one side; the side with the damaged eye.

"How are you feeling?" asked Creighton.

Armbrust tried to rise, but was driven back down by the thundering pain in his head. "I've felt better."

Creighton watched as Falken approached. "I have something that might make you feel better." TC reached for the blouse of a man who was now standing out of Armbrust's line of sight. With a jerk, he flung the captive to the opening of the MTV.

"Recognize this asshole!" said Creighton.

Major Jan Kaspar stood with his shirt stripped from his body. A bandage covered his ear where Shona's blade had severed it in one smooth stroke.

Armbrust's good eye focused in a laser-hard stare. He tried to move, but again the pain drove him back onto the stretcher. He lay there, feeling no pity for the bastard.

"Is this the man who did that to you?" asked Creighton.

Armbrust nodded.

TC's fist snapped with a quick backhand punch. Kaspar's nose exploded; a stream of dark blood ran from his nostrils to his throat.

"That's no way to treat a prisoner, Captain Creighton," a voice called.

Creighton looked up to see Eliason approach. The doctor's daughter walked at his side.

"Have you ever heard of the Geneva Convention, captain?" Eliason asked.

TC thought for a moment. "Yes. Wasn't that the doctrine on the rules of warfare requiring civilized nations to act civilized against their enemy, but that the enemy could act uncivilized against them?"

Eliason suppressed a smile. "Not exactly. However, it did outline the rules for treatment of prisoners. Among other things."

"That was before the Cataclysm," Creighton pointed out. "You are a product of pre-Cataclysm. I'm a product *of* Cataclysm. I don't believe there's much chance you and I are going to agree on too many aspects of how to conduct warfare."

"I'm afraid I never agreed on the conducting of warfare during my time either. I find war to be a senseless undertaking."

Creighton looked at Kaspar, then at Armbrust. He pointed at the Marauder while talking to Eliason. "Perhaps you'd like to explain that to this piece of garbage. Look what he did to one of my men. Not to mention the others he murdered after infecting them with a germ. Is that covered in your Geneva Convention?"

"It was."

Creighton shook his head in amazement. "My God. I read about people like you in school. You were a part of the old world. You ran around spouting peace and love. Brotherhood of man. What was it you were called?"

Eliason straightened proudly. "We were called peace activists. There were millions of us in the world."

Creighton nodded. "That's right. Peace activists. There *were* millions. The Cataclysm took a toll on your enrollment. Now . . . you've become extinct. Like most of the things that were once part of your world."

"They can exist again."

Creighton looked at Kaspar. "I don't think so, Dr. Eliason. This is a different world. There are no gray areas. Everything is black and white. There's no brotherhood of man. No peace activists because there is no peace. There is only us . . . and them."

A deep sadness came over Eliason. "I'm sorry you feel that way, captain."

Creighton's hackles were now up. He thought it necessary to tune the man from the past into the frequency of the present.

"Don't you feel sorry for me. Pity is something I don't need. You chose to miss the trip through the Cataclysm. You rode out Hell in a safe cocoon while the rest of the world suffered the worst fate imaginable. You used to have a saying . . . 'let's have lunch.' Well, by God, my father was slaughtered in the desert and turned into lunch by hostiles. My wife was butchered by Marauders . . . and her eyeballs were torn from her head and eaten! I've seen lunch . . . Cataclysm style."

"I know it must have been difficult," he said softly.

A crazy sort of laughter rippled from Creighton. " 'Difficult'! No, doctor . . . it was *good*! It was good to destroy the bastards who had destroyed my people. Good to watch them die, knowing that the more who died brought us closer to the end. And we were at the end, in America. The end was there. Cataclysm was over. Then we were sent here."

Eliason asked, "Was that really necessary?"

Creighton pointed at Kaspar. "This bastard and his people have to be stopped. That's why we've come. To stop it. Then, just maybe, there might be a place for your kind in the new world. But for now . . . there's only the fight. That's the legacy of your world. That's what you and my ancestors did to the world. You gave us the Cataclysm. And by God, I won't listen to you tell me how to deal with the Cataclysm. You don't have the right. You weren't there! *We were!*"

★★★★★★★★★★★★

Chapter Twenty-three

★★★★★★★

2000.

Colonel Forchette departed the bivouac with the squadrons of MNF tanks and IFV's under her command. According to the map, the Marauders would be forced through a narrow valley in the northeast sector of Quadrant One if they were to attack on the flank. The valley would be where Forchette would be waiting. Which meant an all-night full-throttle march to reach the valley. She shook hands with Creighton and climbed into her tank.

An hour later, the bivouac was settling into the night defense. A few lamps were on, lighting the area.

Creighton was sitting beside his tank, watching the moon; the stars burned brightly, even a soft breeze moved across the desert, creating tiny cyclonic swirls that danced crazily, then disappeared.

His thoughts were on Silver. He took a photograph from his pocket and studied her face. Then a voice called over his shoulder.

"She's beautiful, captain."

Without looking, Creighton recognized the voice of his visitor. "Thank you, Dr. Eliason."

"May I join you?"

Creighton motioned to his side.

Eliason sat in the sand, then said, "Through all

this excitement I haven't thanked you for saving my daughter. I'm very grateful. She's very special to me." He looked at the photograph Creighton was holding. "She's all I have left to remember my wife."

Creighton released a long sigh. "I was pretty hard on you, Dr. Eliason. My apologies. I know you've suffered a great deal. We all have."

They looked up as Roman approached. He was with Shona and Telfi. The three sat down with Creighton and Eliason.

Roman studied Eliason for a long moment, then, as though compelled, said, "Dr. Eliason, you must forgive my inquisitiveness, but you're something of a special find. I've never met anyone who lived prior to the Cataclysm. May I ask you a few questions?"

Eliason nodded politely. "You may."

"This may sound rather naive, but what was earth like? I mean, what did it look like before the Cataclysm?"

Eliason didn't have to think hard. It seemed like yesterday that he was in New Mexico. In a sense, he had been there in the recent past.

"What I recall most vividly, before the great droughts began, was the vegetation. The myriad of the color green is the most remarkable remembrance I have. In New Mexico, the landscape was sparse, more so than the Dakotas, or the eastern regions, but the colors were beautiful. Especially the color green. Greens with red, yellow, blue, the entire spectrum. A beautiful sight."

Roman said, "We had beautiful green vegetation in the biospheres. Not as broad as your New Mexico, but beautiful. Though only on the inside, of course."

"And now? It's obvious you can live in the environment. What is being done to replenish the earth's natural flora and fauna?"

"A great many things. Why, at Base Camp One, here in Africa, one of our agronomists is starting a farm. He's already begun planting shrubs brought from the biomes; soon, green will begin to return to Africa."

"A farm? Fascinating. I grew up on a farm. In Iowa," said Eliason.

This seemed to catch them all off guard; it was, after all, the first conversation they had ever had with someone who lived more than a century before.

"That is fascinating, as well. What was life on the farm like?" asked Creighton.

Eliason shrugged. "That was in the early part of the twenty-first century. My family had to struggle, and drought was always a problem, what with the constant depletion of the ozone layer. But we managed to irrigate crops from undersea aquifers. The government spent billions of dollars bringing water up from beneath the earth to feed the farms that were providing food for the United States. The rest of the world was starving as the drought continued."

"From the heat?" added Roman.

"Yes. The heat from the sun couldn't reflect back into the atmosphere and formed a rolling carpet of heat. Which caused the earth to wither. The entire Midwest turned into a dust bowl, like in the early part of the twentieth century."

"I understand that disease had been conquered," said Roman.

"Most disease. The deadliest ones were ultimately eradicated. AIDS. Cancer. Heart disease. Then the drought began producing wholesale plagues as millions began to starve."

"How did you get your equipment to Africa?" Creighton was still curious about that.

"From several points on the African coast. We transported over the Atlantic by ship to ports in Algeria, Libya, Morocco, Ivory Coast. Dozens of ports. The equipment was then transshipped overland by trucks. Some was brought by transport planes."

"And your site wasn't discovered?" Roman found that notion intriguing.

"The catacombs are in a special place. You'll see tomorrow. We're less than a day's march from the site."

"I presume the catacombs are beneath the ground," said Creighton.

"Something like that." Eliason seemed to be hedging, as though he wasn't certain he could fully trust the Americans.

A long, uncomfortable pause followed.

Eliason studied them, finally asking, "I have to know about the Cataclysm."

Roman seemed to have been waiting for the question. A quick glance around the group; all faces appeared willing. The descendants of the Cataclysm survivors nodded at Roman.

The philosopher began slowly, meticulously, as though unfolding some great secret. In a sense, he was.

"The first stages began in 2050."

"We went into the catacombs in 2050," Eliason said reflectively.

Roman continued. "Fairly good timing. Though there wasn't any remarkable environmental change until 2061. Other than changes on the coastal regions. There were those who suggested the governments had been too hasty. Then it began. The poles began melting with such speed there was no time to build protective barriers along the coastal areas. New York City disappeared completely by the year 2065. Floods inundated the coasts. The entire state of Alaska was lost completely, except the higher elevations. With the flood, of course, there was panic. Millions of people were forced inland. This put greater pressure on an already distressed situation.

"The first signs of what we now refer to as the Chaos Period soon began. The rule of law was replaced by the survival of the fittest. Strength ruled over reason. Organized society as you knew it quickly deteriorated into roving bands of what became known as 'hostiles.' Food. Shelter. All forms of life support were controlled by the hostiles."

"Barbaric," Eliason breathed. Creighton couldn't be certain if the man was reacting to the reality, or to the good fortune of those Magi who would not have survived without Eliason's cryogenic alternative. Or both.

Roman continued. "We're not certain, since there is very little historical data of the half century following the Chaos Period. But it's believed the environment became so severely altered that it was virtually impossible for any life form to survive. Temperatures rose to over 150 degrees; there was no precipitation; food certainly couldn't grow, even if there was anyone to do the planting. Life on the outside of the biospheres settled into its own discipline. That is, what was left."

"And then the biosphere inhabitants began to emerge?"

"Certainly. The environment, after over a half century of freedom from pollutants and pressure, began to heal. The ozone layer began to revive. In time there was rain. The environment hasn't completely healed, but it grows healthier with each passing day. And those of us who survived, the 'specials,' are keenly aware of the mistakes of the past and the responsibility of the present."

"The specials began to emerge from the biosphere." Eliason's words were statement, not question. He seemed like a young child eager for learning.

The group suddenly became grim-looking.

Roman's voice was soft, sounding almost shameful. "Yes. The specials began to emerge. That was when the horror became known."

Eliason didn't have to try and understand. He looked at Shona and Telfi and knew neither man was a survivor of the biospheres. "What exactly was the plan? How were the hostiles dealt with?"

"Mostly with death," Creighton said flatly. "They couldn't be approached. They were as deadly as any poisonous snake that ever crawled the earth. For the most part they were cannibalistic. Some tribes even captured others and raised them like cattle. Fattening them up for slaughter."

Eliason appeared to grow ill. His color changed from white to black, black to white.

Creighton explained the government plan to resettle the country. "When it was obvious the Cataclysm was on the back side of its course, the government—what was left of the government—brought together the leaders from the biospheres. A plan was implemented to send out the trained specials to reclaim the country. They knew it would be bloody. Frankly, there was little hope many hostiles would be saved. But if not saved, destroyed in order that those in the biospheres—the specials—could replenish the population and move forward."

"That sounds familiar. Rather like the American West of the 1800s. Instead, it was called Manifest Destiny. Hostiles were killed then in the name of settling the frontier and ridding the earth of savages. Those savages were called Indians."

Roman stared him in the eye. It was obvious the doctor couldn't differentiate between an Indian and a hostile. "The Indians of America were a great and proud nation. They were a great civilization. A culture. What was done to them was done for different reasons than what was done to the hostiles. The hostiles weren't Indians. An Indian could understand reason. Whether they accepted that reasoning or not is another matter. The hostiles didn't have the foggiest notion of reasoning. They ate their own children! How do you reason with someone like that?"

Eliason said nothing. He stood and walked away. The present was obviously not quite what he had hoped. The people of the present were different. He was different. But in many ways there wasn't much change: like the past, man could still find the eloquence to justify the wrongs done to other human beings.

★★★★★★★★★★★★

Chapter Twenty-four

★★★★★★★

Dr. Phillip Chan had been the principle designer of the catacombs' structural design. A design that was very similar in shape to a pyramid. In a sense, it was a pyramid, with the same intricate passageways, geometric shape, and ironically, the same purpose: an impenetrable tomb. Chan had conceived the idea after a discussion with Dr. Carl Eliason's wife, an archeologist who pointed out the resiliency of pyramids. They were durable, could be built easily enough, and in the desert were not necessarily out of place.

Building the pyramid in secrecy had been the greatest challenge. This meant building the pyramid, dubbed the "catacombs," in sections and transshipping the sections to the site selected for the erection.

The construction required great secrecy, and a great deal of planning and money. The planning was the least difficult part. High-tech computers had drafted a workable design based on the original model, the pyramids of the Pharoahs. Shipment was not as difficult as some might have thought, not with certain "influences" involved. Through the influences, the greatest obstacle was overcome: financing.

The financing was acquired by the members of the project, whose combined wealth fell miserably short of achieving the goal necessary to finance such an adventure. A benefactor was needed. A bankroll. Which meant approaching someone with the most to lose, and the means to prevent the loss: a rich man who would not be invited into the biosphere.

Paul Macur was such a man, and after exhausting every means known to the scientists and others in the project, Macur was given a convincing scientific briefing that persuaded him the world was indeed about to enter into a Cataclysm, that the government was well aware of the impending doom, and that Macur was to be one of the unfortunate millions left to his own devices.

A rich man, Macur knew his wealth would do him no good as a member of the "outsiders."

Macur liquidated his assets and bankrolled the project of Eliason and Chan. Which included his wife and daughter.

There was one final problem to overcome: how to carry out the project in secret, in the Sahara Desert, without gaining worldwide attention.

Macur was the one who came up with the solution: the best means of protecting a secret is to make the secret public knowledge. This came in the form of a commercial venture.

Thus began the "Land of the Pharoahs," a Macur Enterprises business venture to be built in the Sahara Desert featuring a luxurious resort complex modeled after the pyramids of Egypt. Swimming pools, tennis courts, golf courses, a small airstrip, all the facial requirements of a resort were built into the plans, which the Algerian government was eager to support. Especially when several of the leaders of the country were informed of the true nature of the future, and the natural inevitability that was approaching.

Eliason and several geologists located a sandstone strata in the Sahara Desert which would serve as the foundation of the pyramid. The layer of strata began at 300 feet beneath the desert and extended downward another 500 feet, covering an area of over eighty square miles. After excavating 300 feet beneath the desert, the foundation was laid. Onto the foundation was built a pneumatic base that could raise and lower the pyramid. Once the pyramid was built, the structure could be lowered into the "sarcophagus," as the deep pit was called. The wind and sand would cover the last traces of the pyramid. More important, the structure would be safe from probing eyes or wandering outsiders seeking refuge.

The maintenance crews, operating at intervals of five years, would maintain and oversee the function of the pyramid during its hibernation during the Cataclysm. Air was brought in from the surface through periscopelike intakes that could be extended through the surface; the air, though contaminated, could be purified and wasn't needed in great quantities, since the number of living humans was limited. Food was easily stored for the one-hundred-year march through time; food that was mostly dehydrated.

Electrical requirements were the most important. In the desert, it was decided, the greatest natural provider of energy was the sun. A sun that would eventually burn hotter and hotter. A sun that would serve as a greater deterrant against outsiders. All knew that when the Cataclysm began, the last place people would seek relief from the heat would be the hottest place on the face of the planet.

Solar energy had been perfected by 2030, and a series of solar panels, panels that could be raised and lowered from a few feet beneath the surface, would provide the energy needed to run the generators providing energy to the pyramid.

One day, a year after the completion of the pyramid, in 2050, all the reservations were booked. The guests were quietly resting in their rooms; rather, their cryogenic chambers.

Suddenly, and without warning, late one night the Land of the Pharoahs slid quietly beneath the surface of the Sahara.

The frozen journey into the future had begun beneath the sweltering heat of the Sahara Desert.

★★★★★★★★★★★★★

Chapter Twenty-five

★★★★★★★

"Incredible. Absolutely incredible!" Roman Standish stared wide-eyed at the structure in the distance. From the desert rose a tall pyramid; nothing remained around the exterior grounds as described by Eliason. The swimming pools, tennis courts, airstrip—everything was either covered by the sand that had drifted over the site for a century, or was covered by surface sand as the great structure had pushed its way through the surface from beneath the desert.

Creighton had seen nothing like the pyramid in his lifetime, except in the computer library while a student.

The column of tanks moved forward, cutting through the desert until reaching the base of the pyramid. The exterior was composed of polycarbonate glass; bullet- and impact-resistant glass of the same type used to construct biospheres. The structure was designed to withstand the impact of an artillery round.

"The only contingent we didn't plan for was travel," said Eliason, who was riding on the turret of Creighton's tank. "We have the means to construct solar dune buggies, as they were called in my era."

"Is that why you went after your daughter on foot?" asked Creighton.

"Exactly. We were working on the units when she and the other children were taken captive. The children are allowed to play outside under the supervision of adults. They were playing soccer when the Marauders struck. Our security measures require sealing the pyramid if there's a threat from the outside."

"Even if your children are threatened?" asked Creighton.

"Under all circumstances," Eliason replied icily.

Approaching the structure, Creighton could see dozens of people scurrying for what appeared to be an entrance. The people were all dark skinned, indicating they were frightened of the tank column.

"You had better let me go ahead," Eliason urged. "I'm afraid they are confused by the appearance of your column."

Eliason dropped from the tank and walked to the entrance of the structure. From his pocket he took a small communicator and began talking. Minutes later the entrance reopened. Another man appeared. He was not dark skinned. His skin was the color of an Oriental.

Creighton watched curiously. Suddenly, he thought he saw Eliason weaken, as though he were about to faint. Creighton hurried to join the two men.

Phillip Chan watched suspiciously as Creighton approached. The scientist said nothing. He merely nodded.

"What's the problem?" Creighton asked Eliason.

Eliason's eyes shifted, and his voice wavered as he said, "The people you call Marauders . . . they have escaped with the children. They ambushed the men sent to follow their column."

"Dead?"

Eliason nodded. "Their bodies were discovered by another group sent out later. They were tortured to death."

Creighton's facial features never flinched. He remembered his wife. He remembered Forchette's fiancé, who had died at the hands of the Moroccs. "The bastards like to torture people."

Looking at Chan, the tank commander asked, "How far from here were your people discovered?"

"We had one dune buggy operational. The driver estimates twenty kilometers."

"Were there any tracks indicating their direction of march from where the bodies were discovered?"

Chan pointed to the north. "Our driver said they were moving on a line to the north."

"They're heading for the east flank of Quadrant One."

Chan was visibly shaken, and distraught. His skin began to change color. Then he looked at Creighton. "Who is this man? Who are these people?"

"We're Americans," Creighton answered.

Chan stared at him incredulously. Before he could speak, there was a voice from the entrance to the pyramid.

"What do you intend to do about this, Dr. Eliason? My daughter was one of the children captured by those bastards."

Paul Macur stood at the entrance. He carried an automatic weapon Creighton recognized as a popular military type used prior to the Cataclysm.

Beside Macur stood another person. A woman. She had dark hair and deep-blue eyes. She appeared to be in her early twenties.

"The man is Paul Macur. The woman is Dana Macur. She's Macur's wife."

Creighton and the woman's eyes locked momentarily.

Macur hurried forward. "What do you intend to do?" he demanded.

Creighton stared past the face of Macur; past his flaming red eyes to the woman.

"We're going to get them back," Creighton whispered to the woman.

PART THREE IRON HORSE

★★★★★★★★★★★★★

Chapter Twenty-six

★★★★★★★

Base Camp One was buzzing. The excitement was electrical, supercharging the AfriKorps soldiers with anticipation few had known. None present were more excited than Colt Derider, who had arrived shortly after sunrise from the southern survey mission. He had reached camp tired and dirty and wanting a hot shower. That's when Colonel Clayton told him the Iron Horse, as the train was called, was now on track and preparing for its maiden run through the desert of Africa.

Forgetting the shower, Derider hurried with Clayton to the roundhouse, where the sleek train was being assembled. He arrived in time to find Nick Ruhland, the engineer, going through the computerized systems check of the engine.

Ruhland was a big man with dark hair and eyes, and huge hands; hands that moved smoothly, even gently over the computer keyboard. Like Derider, his world was the world of trains. He had driven the first train from the Omaha Biosphere to Reno on its initial shakedown run. Given the opportunity to bring the train to Africa, he volunteered instantly. The journey across the ocean was the worst; Ruhland was seasick for most of the time, but survived by keeping his thoughts centered on his duty: bring the train to Derider.

Wearing a broad grin, Ruhland approached Derider. "She's ready for a trial run. All systems are up and running."

Derider couldn't hide his jubilation. "What about the weapons systems?"

Derider and Clayton followed Ruhland to the engine. The engine was bullet shaped; on the sides were weapons platforms integrated into the hull of the engine. On the nose, another weapons system could pop out from its concealed station. The weapons were mostly rockets, with the exception of the nose system. The nose weapons platform was a .30mm six-barreled chain gun. The uranium depleted bullets were armor piercing and could reduce a tank to scrap metal in an instant.

Trailing in tandem behind the main engine were several fortress cars, heavily armed platforms that provided flank protection to the train. Included in the string of platforms were a mess car and a hospital car where surgery could be performed.

The most impressive platform was what Derider called the "hunter" platform. The platform was armed with multiple-warhead image-seeking missiles capable of being launched, seeking a target based on a computerized image, and either killing the target acquisitioned, or if no target was found, returning to the launch platform where the missiles could be recovered, rearmed if necessary, and redeployed.

From other cars infantry fighting vehicles could be loaded and deployed down ramps. More than a dozen cars were designed to deploy MBT's. And there were four cars designated as the armory.

The rear car was not a caboose, the traditional work car of the train. Instead, there was an exact replica of the front engine compartment, complete with weapons systems. The train could fight in either of two forward directions while putting out full-fire suppression on the flanks from the platforms.

"Beautiful," Clayton said in a stage whisper.

"She's one high-stepping, fighting lady, colonel," said Ruhland. Then there was a gleam in his eye as he looked at Derider. "And she's ready for her first dance in Africa."

"Fire her up," Derider ordered.

Ruhland went to the forward compartment where he pressed the keys of the digital keyboard on the outside of the compartment. There was a slight whirring sound, then the compartment unfolded like a clamshell. The three men climbed inside where they strapped themselves into contoured leather seats. Ruhland sat at the control panel marked ENGINEER. Clayton sat watching.

Momentarily, the engine began moving as the solar-powered train started along the track.

The train moved slowly from the roundhouse through the camp, causing quite a commotion. Nomads ran as the train glided along the track; soldiers stood in awe at the procession of engine and weapons platforms. At the edge of camp a guard opened the gate of the security fence and the Iron Horse glided out of the security of the camp.

"Hang on," Ruhland said in a calm voice.

His fingers punched computer buttons, and like a shot, the train streaked along the track.

The speed built increasingly as Ruhland punched other buttons on the power computer. Within minutes the train was travelling at nearly 150 miles per hour.

"This is unbelievable," said Clayton.

Derider looked at the tank commander. Clayton wore the same smiling expression as Derider had when, as a child, his father gave him his first electrical toy train in the Omaha Biosphere.

Across the flat terrain the Iron Horse rode, on tracks laid on raised roadbeds by engineers brought to the African continent in the last three months.

"Take us to end of line," Derider ordered.

Ruhland set the power to maximum. Clayton felt nothing, but through the porthole windows on the side he could see the desert flash by. Passing through an MNF position, he barely caught a glimpse of the tanks guarding one of the outposts located near the frontier of Quadrant One.

★★★★★★★★★★★★★★

Chapter Twenty-seven

★★★★★★★

Two hours later, the train was travelling nearly 200 miles per hour when Ruhland began backing off the power; the decrease was gradual, causing no more than a tug against Clayton's shoulder straps. But he could see the train was coming to a very fast halt.

When forward motion had stopped, Derider unbuckled his straps and stepped to the clamshell door. He pressed a button and the bright light of the sun boiled into the compartment as the clamshell opened.

"Here we are, colonel. End of line."

The three men stepped down from the engine; the heat was rising, causing the three to perspire as they walked toward a work crew fifty meters to the front of the engine.

A squad of two IFV's and four MBT's provided security for the track-laying crew.

Unlike their predecessors of three centuries past, the work gang was not composed of graders, pick-and-shovelers, track layers, and spike drivers.

The process of raising and grading the bed, which rose four feet from the surface, laying crossties, then laying and joining track was done by one autonomous unit affectionately called "Roadbed Ruthie."

Ruthie was a large contraption that moved across the surface, gouging up sand, which was then conveyed through a heat compactor that literally turned the sand into liquid. The liquid sand was mixed with a rapid-cooling chemical, then channeled into the groove at the center of the machine. Once the liquid was poured, the setting process followed almost instantly; however, before the cooling process was complete, crossties were implanted into the planed surface. The next step was the placement of interlocking tracks onto the ties.

Track was laid at the rate of five miles per hour. Track that would never have to be repaired.

Like a giant snail leaves its slimy trail across the earth, Ruthie left her trail in the form of a continuous track of shiny rails.

Walking alongside Ruthie, Derider explained to Clayton the rapid deployment aspect of Ruthie. "She can go just about anywhere, colonel. She can cut through new territory at will with limited survey, especially flat terrain, like the Eastern Quadrant."

"What about mountains?" He knew there were a lot of mountains to cross in the move south.

"We only need to bring along prefabricated bridging. That is made at Base Camp One in the roundhouse. Actually, it's slower than the actual grading and track laying. But it can be done rather quickly and efficiently."

"What about sabotage?"

Derider shook his head. "The roadbed is impervious to any type of conventional explosive. The bed is harder than steel once the sand is processed and compacted. The tracks can't be removed, so there's no chance of digging up the track."

"What about planting explosives on the track? The train could be blown off the track."

Derider grinned at Ruhland, who answered the question. "The entire course of the tracks is treaded with thermal imaging sensors. Tampering with the track will relay the exact location to the control center in the engine. The tracks can either be electrified, killing and clearing the track of intruders, or identifying the location, in which case the train is automatically stopped before the detonating point."

"That could still put the train in a sensitive position for ambush."

Ruhland swept his arms toward the awesome firepower arrayed in the platforms positioned between the two fighting engine houses. "I hope they try. They'll find out what Hell looks like."

"What about nomads? Some could wander onto the track. We don't want to kill innocent people who are on our side."

A coldness settled into Ruhland's eyes. "I promised you a perfect fighting machine, colonel. Not perfection in every sense of the word. From the engine the operator can observe the thermal image and determine if it's people crossing the track—or people fucking with the track. If it's intruders—the tracks can be electrified! If I were you I would get the word out to the nomads that if they cross the track . . . do so expeditiously."

Clayton figured he was right. "What about maintenance on the track?"

"What we call a 'pig.' Anything goes wrong, we send the pig down the line. The pig carries a maintenance crew. Sand drifts are no problem, the engine has a modern version of a cowcatcher on the nose. We can plow through drifts thirty feet high at full speed. Fifty feet high at half speed. I don't believe drifts will get higher than that. If so, we'll find a way through."

Clayton was thoroughly impressed. Judging where he stood, the edge of Quadrant One was only a few miles in the distance. In a matter of days the entire Eastern

Quadrant could be rapidly deployed with squadrons of MBT's, hundreds of IFV's, and thousands of troops.

A deployment that could be facilitated within hours.

"Let's return to base," Clayton ordered.

They mounted from the rear end. The Iron Horse streaked from the end of the track; within seconds, the sleek fighting train had disappeared to the west.

Away from the probing eyes of a man who had observed the train with the same astonishment as his enemy.

★★★★★★★★★★★★★

Chapter Twenty-eight

★★★★★★★

Captain Curt Veries wiped at the sweat running along his sun browned features. Behind the binoculars, his green eyes were focusing on the strange contraption churning through the desert, leaving a raised platform in its wake that paved the way for what was in his mind the most unusual machine he had ever seen. He knew the machine was a train. He had seen pictures of such machines on the computer screens of his southern homeland.

Veries's tank and three other Leopards were pulled in behind a long dune stretching along the base of a mountain range to the south. A recon element, Veries had been sent from the base camp to reconnoiter the European defenses at the frontier. What he saw was yet another obstacle appearing in their battle plan.

He checked his watch and again yelled at the radioman in his tank. "Have you made contact with Colonel Motti?"

The radioman called back from inside the tank, "Yes. He wants you on the radio."

Veries explained the situation, the sighting of the train and the advancing track.

He heard his orders, then buttoned up inside the tank. Rolling away, he was relieved he had been ordered to report to the staging camp.

More plans would be needed to continue the move on the European flank.

Plans that would, no doubt, include the use of the thirty children captured last week by their forces.

Plans that would include the use of the bacteria transported to the column from the rear.

★★★★★★★★★★★★

Chapter Twenty-nine

★★★★★★★

Dana Macur had led Creighton and his men on a tour through the pyramid, which was layer upon layer of rooms Spartanly furnished. The lighting was ancient by biosphere standards, as was the texture of the walls; the facilities were reminiscent of a bygone era. A bygone century.

"Fascinating," Roman had remarked. "Like a walk back into history."

Afterwards, Creighton and the others were in a meeting room fed by air conditioning. Macur appeared intent on commanding the discussion. His features had settled from the emotionally strange state to that of his normal appearance. He had gray hair and cold gray eyes that looked like ball bearings. They didn't move, except to leer.

"Our children are still in the hands of those bastards, Eliason." There was the hint of accusation in the statement, suggesting Eliason should be held responsible for his failure to recover the children.

"I'm sorry, Paul. I did my best," was Eliason's only reply.

"You found your child. But what about mine?"

"I found his child," snapped Falken.

"Blaming people won't help, Mr. Macur," said Roman. "What we have is a plan of action. We have our own people moving in that direction at this very moment. But you must understand, whatever Captain Creighton does is for the good of the entire operation. You can't expect him to jeopardize an entire operation for a few. Even though they are children."

"My God," said Macur. "You bastards really are a bunch of coldblooded sonsabitches. You act like the death of thirty children is nothing but a notation on a balance sheet."

"In a sense it is, Mr. Macur," Roman said as gently as possible. "You haven't seen the things we've seen. You haven't had death become a part of your life with such regularity of occurrence as have we. I understand your feelings. But believe me, we are talking to you in the only language the world presently understands."

"Who are those bastards? Renegades from a biosphere, no doubt."

"Renegades? Hardly. According to what Eliason learned they're former hostiles who overpowered a biosphere and learned the technology. Now they're rolling up Africa *en route* to Europe. That's why we're here. To push them south and destroy them."

"Can you do that?" asked Macur.

"You better believe it," said Puhaly. "Those tin cans are junk compared to our equipment. But they play dirty. They have already used kids to kill a group of our people."

"How?" The thought was obviously scaring Macur; he was changing again to the darker shade.

Creighton explained what had happened to Armbrust's patrol.

"My God," Macur breathed. Dana tried to comfort him but he still remained in his emotionally accented state.

"Which means," added Eliason, "they may use our children for the same purposes."

Creighton and Falken looked at each other. They seemed to be thinking the same thought.

Forchette!

"Reno . . . get on the horn!" Creighton ordered.

★★★★★★★★★★★★★

Chapter Thirty

★★★★★★★

Colonel Forchette was at the lead of the two squadrons moving north along the edge of a mountain range that stood as a barrier against the Sahara Desert. The voice of a lieutenant in an IFV came over the radio, reporting something strange.

"I see a child. Damned if the child doesn't look like the one we had in our bivouac with Creighton."

Forchette's instincts came alive. The instincts a woman has for a child lost in the desert. The way she was once lost in the desert.

"Recover the child and return to my position."

She waited. Instead of hearing the voice of the lieutenant, she heard another familiar voice. "Colonel Forchette . . . this is Reno Falken. Be advised . . . there may be children in your sector being used as contamination carriers. Repeat. There may be children in your sector being used as contamination carriers."

Forchette didn't respond. Instead, she ordered the tank forward, then took her microphone. "Do not approach the child. Repeat. Do not approach the child. The child may be contaminated."

There was no answer.

The young IFV officer stood watching the child. He felt a pang of heartache as he saw the dark-skinned child of no more than eight struggle to walk toward him. The pain in the flaming red eyes was made more tragic by the stream of tears running down her face.

"Lieutenant," a voice shouted from the IFV. "Colonel Forchette, sir. She says not to approach the child. The child may be contaminated with a virus."

The lieutenant was young, but he understood the need to follow orders; he understood that the welfare of the many was more important than the welfare of the few.

But the child didn't understand. The child was of another century. A cruel century, for certain. But one that had given her the love of a father and mother. Something the children of this century, particularly in this part of the world, didn't understand.

Seeing the men retreat to the steel protection of the IFV, the child raced to the vehicle, and felt bewildered as the IFV stormed away, spewing dust in the air. Leaving her wondering why she was being treated so cruelly.

Her head ached; her eyes throbbed. Her mouth was dry and there was a great pain in her stomach.

Finally, she could stand no more. She lay in the sand and her thoughts drifted to the man with gray hair and gray eyes. To the woman with long dark hair and dancing blue eyes.

She shuddered. Then she heard the hum of another vehicle approaching. A woman was suddenly standing in front of her. She looked like her mother, with the same brown hair and laughing blue eyes. Eyes that brimmed with tears.

She reached for her mother, or the woman she thought was her mother, and for the first time in her life found herself rejected by the woman who gave her birth.

That was the worst tragedy. Worse than the pain. Worse than the heat.

Again she shuddered and thought she heard the woman cry out something in a language she didn't understand. Then her dark skin turned white; her red eyes became gray; her white hair turned a deep brown. And the pain in her head and stomach was gone.

As was the life of Christina Macur.

★★★★★★★★★★★★★

Chapter Thirty-one

★★★★★★★

"Dead? How can you be certain it was Christina? It could have been any of the children. There were thirty children, for Chrissakes!" Paul Macur was defending the final ground a father had in facing the death of a child: certainty of identification. It gave hope where otherwise there would be total despair; momentary respite from agony that would be eternal.

Creighton slumped in a chair in the meeting room where several of the AfriKorps personnel were gathered. The message from Forchette had provided a means of identification. What was needed was the bona fide.

"Did your daughter have a tiny scar over her left eyebrow?" Creighton asked softly.

Macur said nothing, except a deep, guttural moan that made TC's skin crawl; made his heart ache.

"Did she wear a gold bracelet on her left wrist? The inscription said, 'To Christina . . . from daddy.' "

Again the groan and there was little doubt that the child was his daughter.

The room quickly emptied, and Macur sat alone with his wife. His second wife. A wife who didn't fully understand the pain of losing a child. He thought of what was only months before, but which was in reality more than a century.

His daughter and he had splashed in the swimming

pool of the resort; the swimming pool was gone. So was his daughter. He recalled their playing tennis, and how her backhand had made him realize the youth in his legs was fading. As her life had faded into the darkness of death.

When a man goes insane with grief, it's not a gradual withering process. Rather, it happens almost instantly. Nature's cocoon, protective, allowing the insane the dignity of going into their new world quickly. Carrying only the pain that brought about the disease.

Macur went insane within minutes of learning of his daughter's death. Gone was his ability to reason as sane men are capable of reasoning. Gone was his compassion; replaced by the hunger that needed to be fed:

Revenge!

★★★★★★★★★★★★★★★

Chapter Thirty-two

★★★★★★★★

Major Jan Kaspar had been taken to a room in the lower level of the pyramid. He had been treated fairly, a display he wasn't certain was sincere, or a form of subterfuge to exact information he had thus far refused to divulge. Torture was something he had been trained to withstand. Torture he knew, where information was the goal, was designed to frighten; to intimidate. The torture could only go so far, otherwise, the subject would die and the information would be lost forever.

On the other hand, torture for the sheer pleasure of torture was another matter. That torture was meant to give the administrator of torture a form of pleasure he had yet to find equalled either in combat, or in bed with a woman.

Like the torture of Armbrust. To destroy his eye was merely to prepare him for the ultimate torture, after he had done as instructed. He had planned to drive the man's tank over his spreadeagled body the way he had done to the nomad in the village in the valley at the edge of the Sahara.

That would be torture for pleasure!

He was sitting in a chair with his eyes covered; his hands were tied behind his back with a rope. Every sound caught his attention, and when he heard and felt the vacuum rush through the room he knew the door had opened.

Kaspar said nothing. He had figured out these Europeans. They were soft. Had he been on the other side of the table he would have gotten the information he wanted. He knew how to get information.

Suddenly, he jerked upright. He felt a hand grasp his shoulder. Blinded by the cloth covering his eyes, he felt his body being pulled through the dark world

"What do you want?" he asked.

There was no answer.

Again the question, which began to sound like a plea.

Still no answer.

There was only the heavy breathing. And an occasional sound, like a cry that rose from the stomach but was caught in the mouth, then swallowed.

An aching sound.

The sound of another door opening followed. Then another. Suddenly, he was sitting again. The surface was soft. The blindfold was removed from his eyes and he tried to look at his handler, but before his eyes could focus there was only the vision of a man's back hurrying through a door.

There was a small window in the door. Momentarily, the face of a man appeared in the window.

The face of a madman! he thought. Such eyes. The eyes of insanity. Eyes he had seen so many times before on the faces of people he had tortured.

Then the face was gone.

Paul Macur sat at the control panel operating the cryogenic chamber that held captive one of the men he blamed for his daughter's death.

He turned on the unit; a humming noise followed. When ready, he turned a dial controlling the temperature.

He set the temperature at zero degrees Fahrenheit.

Kaspar felt the temperature of the room begin to drop. At first the temperature was comfortable, cool, even pleasant.

Then there was the crispness in his breathing; frosty clouds began to appear with each expelled breath.

The pain became worse until he felt himself begin to ache as the cold worked into his bones. He tried to move, and felt something snap at his right knee.

He tried to scream, but his lungs couldn't issue the sound. It was as though the alveoli had crystallized in his lungs, and there was a deep metallic taste in his mouth.

Then he understood the absurdity: in the Sahara Desert, one of the hottest places on the face, or beneath, the planet earth, he was freezing to death!

His eyes turned up to the window; he felt his eyelids crack as the muscles moved the lids, allowing him to see the face staring maniacally at him.

He recognized the face, which was black, the hair white, the eyes flaming red with a demonic glow.

It is the father of one of the children.

Then Major Jan Kaspar, a man who never had shown compassion to a single soul on earth, felt the blood in his veins coagulate like a river of cooling lead.

In the next instance, guided by his insanity, Paul Macur reached to the panel and turned another dial. This set the temperature in the adjoining chamber to minus fifty degrees Fahrenheit.

He walked into the chamber with resolve, closed the door, then sat on the reclined chair.

The air turned cold; his breath grew crisp, heavy white splotches that drifted then disappeared.

He thought he saw the face of his daughter; heard her voice, but it was only the insanity.

Again.

Or was it the guilt?

He had brought his child to the other side of the world, defied nature by sheltering her from the natural order of things for over a century. In trying to preserve her life, he had mutated it, then caused her death.

He had tried to defy nature, and knew as the life raced from his body that he had no right to be here.

He should have endured the Cataclysm. Even in that Hell, he might have found more life with his daughter than he had by robbing nature.

★★★★★★★★★★★★★

Chapter Thirty-three

★★★★★★★

Creighton watched Dana Macur as her husband's body was removed from the cryogenic chamber. She was stoic; robotlike as she touched his frozen hand. But what struck Creighton as odd was that there wasn't the remorse of a fresh widow. Then, as though she were reading his thoughts, she said, "The love had drained from our marriage years ago. But he was a wonderful father. He adored his daughter."

"His daughter?" Creighton asked.

She nodded. "Christina was his daughter by a previous marriage. Spoiled rotten, but a lovely child." A tear rolled down her cheek.

"What are your plans?" asked Creighton.

She thought for a moment. "Am I still considered an American citizen?"

Creighton nodded. "Certainly. Why?"

"I would like to return to the United States. You said the government is rebuilding the country. Repopulating."

"That is true. I'm certain you would be invaluable."

"Invaluable? In what way?"

"You were there before the Cataclysm. It's as though only yesterday you were watching it happen. You knew our country. What it looked like. The beauty. The history. You would be a valuable teaching resource. All of you, as a matter of fact. I'm certain the government would be eager to have you share your knowledge with the country."

"What about the violence?"

He shook his head. "The violence is all but over. Only here . . . and in other countries, perhaps. But the United States is practically tame. And the grass is coming back. Trees are growing again. Rivers are flowing. Lakes are filling now that rain has returned."

"Rain?"

He smiled. "Rain. It's the damndest thing I've ever seen. Water falling from the sky. Just like in the biome."

She remembered something. "When I was young, I loved to walk in the rain. To feel the water run down my face. Soaking my hair." Which made her suddenly realize something else. "What about our . . ." She paused. Searching for the right words.

Creighton said it for her. "Your 'condition'?"

She laughed. "I've never had a condition before. I suppose that's as good a term as any. Yes. What about our condition? We will look very strange."

Creighton chuckled. "One thing's certain."

"What's that?"

"You won't have any problem letting people know when you're angry."

They both laughed, and she realized something. "I haven't laughed in more than one hundred years."

Creighton realized it was the first time he had laughed with a woman since Silver's death. It felt good. "We need to talk with Eliason. I would imagine a great many of your people may want to return to their countries. But first . . . we have to recover the children."

"Do you think they're alive?"

"They're alive. But I believe I know what they have planned for them. It's a horrible plan."

He explained what he believed the Marauders would do with the children.

"My God!" she gasped. "That's barbaric."

"We're dealing with barbarians."

They left and joined the others in the main meeting room which had served as the lobby area when the pyramid was being used as a resort.

Parents of children were frantic; many were shouting threats at Eliason, who was trying to calm them down.

"Captain Creighton and his forces are going after the children. But the rescue operation must be conducted carefully. Otherwise, the children will be killed. We are not dealing with rational people. These Marauders are vicious and will stop at nothing to reach their objective."

Puhaly came in carrying a field radio pack. Creighton took the handphone and spoke with Forchette. He listened for a moment, then looked at his gunner, telling Puhaly, "Forchette's found the staging area. She estimates nearly 150 tanks are staging for an attack on the eastern flank."

"What about the children?" Eliason asked.

Creighton took a deep breath and it was obvious he didn't want to answer. He took Eliason off to the side amid the suspicious grumblings of the frantic parents.

"The children have been deployed around the staging area perimeter."

"Deployed? What the hell does that mean?"

"It means . . . they've been positioned in the sand as human shields."

Eliason's eyes bulged and his jaw dropped. Then his skin darkened, his hair turned white, and his eyes burned like fire.

Puhaly felt his skin crawl, but he understood the man's anger. He only wished he could get his hands on the bastards.

Puhaly and Creighton talked in private. They nearly had to shout at each other to hear over the din.

"Get everybody saddled up. We're going to hook up with Forchette."

"What about Armbrust? He says he wants to go."

Armbrust was in the Hummer vehicle used by the medical team. "If he can cut it, then he goes. I'll need every tank commander I can get my hands on."

Puhaly glanced at the angry parents. "We have the IFV's from his patrol, but not enough personnel to make the IFV's tactically operational."

Creighton followed the line of Puhaly's sight to the group of parents. "Are you thinking what I'm thinking?"

Puhaly ran one hand over his face, then stared at his palms for a moment. "They're certainly not familiar with our equipment. Especially the weapons systems on the MBT's. But I'm confident they could drive the IFV's and fire the weapons we recovered. Hell, some of these people may have been responsible for the earlier designs. Eliason said a few were former soldiers. And it would give us a larger force. One hundred fifty tanks and infantry . . . man, that's a hellacious force sitting on the eastern flank."

"Get Armbrust and bring him here. If he's fit . . . he goes. Meanwhile, set up a weapons familiarization block of instruction. We roll in two hours."

★★★★★★★★★★★★★★★

Chapter Thirty-four

★★★★★★★★

1330.

Derider and Ruhland were summoned from the roundhouse by Clayton. The C in C was sitting in his mobile command center studying a map of the eastern area of Quadrant One. A red line extended from Base Camp One to the frontier. Where the red line ended was the point Derider had called "end of line." On both sides of the end of line position, high mountains stood as barriers on the north and south approach leading back to Base Camp One.

"End of line, all right," Clayton muttered. "End of the line for those bastards."

Derider and Ruhland entered. Clayton motioned them to chairs surrounding a small table.

"Gentlemen, I think it's time we put your Iron Horse to work."

Derider's features lit up. "What's happening?"

Clayton explained the situation, then laid out the plan he had devised. He went to the map. "Colonel Forchette has radioed her position. She's here." He pointed at a position southeast of end of line, at the eastern base of a mountain range. Then he moved the pointer to the east, over what was approximately fifty kilometers from the roadbed crew. "There is a

Marauder staging area here. More than 150 tanks. A full division."

Ruhland released a long whistle. "What about infantry?"

"Approximately 2,500 ground-support troops."

"Where did they come from?" asked Ruhland.

Clayton shrugged. "Where doesn't matter. They are here. And there's another problem. The people you stumbled across . . . the people from the twenty-first century? Their children have been taken hostage and are being used as shields around the staging area. Forchette is in radio range with Creighton and reports Creighton's elements are moving to join with her element."

"That'll seal the rear retreat," Derider noted.

"Precisely. Which leaves the Marauders only one of two directions . . . east, into the desert, where we can dog and bleed them to death. Or west. Toward our position."

"The track-laying team," Ruhland gasped. "My God. They'll be slaughtered."

Clayton flashed a mean grin. "Not if your train can do everything you say it can do. The MBT's providing security will get your people out when the time is right."

Derider understood. "You're going to use them as bait." It wasn't a question.

"That's exactly what I'm going to do. The advance has to pass right through end of line. Forchette has been ordered to hold her position and wait for Creighton. They'll hook up and swing into a blocking position here." He ran his finger along a line extending west to east from the base of the mountain range west of the Marauder staging area.

"You know what that creates, don't you, colonel," said Ruhland.

Derider studied the plan and the terrain. He also understood what was going to happen.

Clayton clapped his hands resoundingly. "I do, sir. It creates the classic tank battle!"

★★★★★★★★★★★★★★

Chapter Thirty-five

★★★★★★★★

Captain Curt Veries walked past the sentry posted at the tent of divisional headquarters. Veries paused before going through the flap and glanced toward the perimeter which he couldn't see. But he knew what was out there.

Children.

The thought didn't bother him. Rather, he considered the ploy in a more practical sense. A thought he expressed moments later with the division commander, Colonel Ansel Motti.

Motti was built like a cube; his face was cubelike, his chest barrellike, his shoulders square. He had blond hair that was close-cropped and green eyes that stared menacingly at whomever he spoke.

"From what we've learned about the Europeans, they will be more hardened by the use of the children. I recommend you shoot the little bastards. Bury them and leave no trace. By doing what you propose they will fight that much harder. It seems to be their way."

Compassion was a quality that Motti didn't understand. A tough and ruthless veteran of the drive north from the southern tip of Africa, Motti had started as a captain, like Veries. His face, which resembled a scarred bulldog, turned even harsher as he listened to the advice. Advice he quickly dismissed.

"Fuck the Europeans' sense of outrage and morality. The children will stay where they are. If their reconnaissance units have located our position, they will be less eager to attack. If not, we'll deploy the children as planned. What you had better be concerned with is the success of your mission tonight. If you're not successful, there'll be no battle. We'll have to withdraw. If we do . . . we'll bury the little bastards beneath our treads."

Motti went to a map on a folding table erected in the center of the tent. He touched the spot on the map where the railroad track ended in the desert.

Then he thought about the superiority of the European tanks, especially those of the troops his intelligence sources called Americans. What angered him most was the recurring failures plaguing the battle plan.

"Your plan to infect the Europeans with the virus failed, Veries. As Kaspar has no doubt failed to capture one of the enemy tanks."

Veries shrugged. "It was a good plan. Plans often fail. The European officer refused to get near the child. Which means they must know what happened with Kaspar's patrol. Have you heard from Kaspar?"

Motti shook his head. "The bastard is probably dead." His eyes narrowed. "Failure is not acceptable. Is your unit prepared for your mission tonight?"

"Yes, sir."

Motti nodded approvingly. Veries was a good soldier; a little too lenient, but that would change as he faced more battles. Motti had once been soft himself. But no longer. He knew what had to be done and how to achieve an end.

"Don't fail, Veries. Succeed. Or die where you fail. There will be no reason for you to return to this camp if you fail."

Veries left and walked to where his tank platoon was stationed inside the perimeter. The six Leopard tanks were drawn up tight; canvas was strung between two to make a shaded area. Four of his tank commanders sat beneath the canvas.

The subject of their attention was a filthy nomad woman discovered in the foothills the day before. She had been stripped naked and was huddled against the treads of a tank.

Veries looked at her contemptuously, then at his tank commanders. "When you're finished with the slut, cut her throat and bury her. We have a briefing in one hour."

Veries walked off to the laughter of his men; to the screams of the woman. His thoughts were on what he had waiting in his tent.

★★★★★★★★★★★★★★

Chapter Thirty-six

★★★★★★★

Erica Chan was tied to the pole supporting the center of the canvas tent. Her body was covered with bruises from the beating administered the day before by Veries, who had taken her from the other children. She was sixteen; the oldest in the group and obviously becoming a woman. It seemed like only yesterday she had been swimming in the pool at the pyramid. Now, she had been kidnapped, beaten, and raped by a vicious bastard who acted as though taking human life were no more important than changing shoes.

When the flap jerked back she stiffened. Veries entered and removed his pistol belt. He was leering at her as he unbuttoned his shirt, then unbuckled his belt.

A chill raced through her body and she felt the emotional reaction frustrating her central nervous system. In seconds, the honey-skinned young woman with long dark hair and deep brown eyes had turned into the mutant state caused during the prolonged stay in the cryogenic chamber.

She didn't resist his overtures. That would be senseless, and would only weaken her further. She had to submit, if for no other reason than to survive.

Survive to do what she could to get her and the other children out of this hellhole.

Survive in order that she, too, might live another hour. Another day.

Survive in order that she might get the opportunity to stick a knife in the throat of this sonofabitch!

★★★★★★★★★★★★★

Chapter Thirty-seven

★★★★★★★

1800.

"I don't like it." Puhaly repeated himself for the third time in the last hour. "I don't like advancing at night. It's too risky. Especially with all these . . . civilians!"

Creighton lowered himself into the seat and closed the hatch. Sitting in a jump seat between Puhaly and Creighton, Eliason ignored the reference to civilians.

"They can shoot, can't they?" Creighton asked.

"Most couldn't hit their ass with both hands," Puhaly replied.

Fergus piped in, "Most people you train to shoot can't hit their asses with both hands. Matter of fact, you can't hit your ass with both hands."

"Fuck you, Fergus. You just drive or I'll shove your ass through this barrel and fire you and show you how accurate I can shoot."

Fergus laughed, then replied, "Power up."

The hum of the solar batteries gave off a steady rhythm.

"Move out," Creighton ordered through the microphone.

At the point, Reno Falken was standing in the turret of his IFV. The air conditioning was turning out a cool stream of air that exhausted through the turret, creating a relaxing flow of air across his body.

He glanced at one of his passengers. Phillip Chan sat looking determined; the fear he might have known in another life had been replaced by the resolve he felt toward recovering his daughter.

The column rolled out with IFV's taking the flanks as security; Falken and his IFV would stay ahead of the convoy, providing reconnaissance and security.

Creighton's tank was at the center, providing the command post for the column.

Eliason's thoughts drifted from the death of Macur to the children, to a fact he had considered only in the last few hours: he had never killed a man before. He had never been in combat nor struck another human being in anger.

And like so many others, he was wondering if perhaps he shouldn't have stayed in the twenty-first century. At least there things were more complicated, which allowed for a person to have a mixture of attitudes. In this century attitudes weren't complicated. Everything was so clear. Attitude was shaped around one basic premise, one shared by Europeans, Americans, nomads, and Marauders: survival.

Which meant that a man had to kill if he was to survive.

And he was going to survive, if for no other reason than for his child.

And he would do whatever it took.

★★★★★★★★★★★★★★

Chapter Thirty-eight

★★★★★★★

2315.

Base Camp One was alive with the activity of loading men, equipment, and supplies onto the Iron Horse. Derider and Ruhland had worked through the day and night getting the weapons systems loaded, computer programmed, and mapping information into the brain of the missile systems.

On the track, MBT's were storming up the ramps of the flatbeds; IFV's were loading onto other flatbeds, while the infantry troops were loading into their bulletproof transit cars.

"What's our ETA to the frontier?" Clayton asked Derider.

"Two A.M., barring any complications."

Clayton checked his watch, then went to the command post where he contacted the European commander of the MNF stationed at the frontier. He issued his orders, showered, then dressed in a fresh uniform.

By midnight the train was fully loaded. In the forward control center of the Iron Horse, Clayton joined Derider and Ruhland.

Clayton settled into his seat and buckled the shoulder harness. Derider would operate the missile system if needed; Ruhland would operate the train.

At 12:15 P.M. the train departed, threading through

the security gate. Outside the camp's perimeter, Ruhland accelerated the train, giving the Iron Horse its first run at full power with a maximum load.

Clayton sat back, closed his eyes, and in his mind began to visualize what he believed would be the greatest tank battle in over 200 years.

★★★★★★★★★★★★

PART FOUR
END OF TRACK

★★★★★★★

★★★★★★★★★★★★★★★

Chapter Thirty-nine

★★★★★★★

0300.

Reno Falken lay hidden behind a dune, staring through night-vision binoculars at a sight that made his stomach turn. Four hundred meters to the front the pitiful image of a child was clear enough, even in the darkness, for the soldier to see how truly treacherous an enemy the AfriKorps was facing.

The child was one of several he could see forming a human necklace in the sand in front of the perimeter; to the rear he could make out enemy tanks dispersed among infantry defense positions. The camp was nearly a mile wide, and from what Falken could see, a mile deep. There were no lights and the camp appeared quiet with the exception of an occasional sentry walking patrol.

"I estimate more than 150 tanks inside the perimeter," Falken whispered to Shona, who lay beside him.

Shona took the binoculars and scanned the staging area. His eyes stopped, riveted on one of the hostage children.

From what he could see the child was tied to a heavy object, anchoring the youngster to the desert floor.

Suddenly, both men froze. The groan of an approaching vehicle drew their attention to the no man's land between the child and where they lay.

"Perimeter security," Falken whispered.

A halftrack vehicle appeared, moving slowly around the perimeter. They watched the vehicle pull to a halt. One of the Marauders got out, relieved himself, then disappeared inside the halftrack. The vehicle continued its patrol, following the worn grooves in the sand marking its course.

Falken checked his watch, timing the return of the vehicle, which he figured was patrolling a certain sector of the perimeter. Five minutes later the vehicle returned.

"I wish to hell we could get inside that camp. We might learn what they have planned."

"There is a way, my friend," Shona whispered.

Through the darkness Falken could see Shona's teeth gleam. "What do you have in mind?"

Shona explained his plan.

Falken looked at him incredulously. "You must be insane!"

Shona touched Falken's shoulder reassuringly. "It will work. Besides, do you have a better plan?"

Falken nearly laughed. "I don't have any plan at all."

"Then we have to try."

"O.K. Let's get back to the IFV. There's some equipment there you'll need."

The two men slithered backwards, then ran in a low crouch toward the IFV parked behind a dune.

Inside the IFV Falken went to a storage compartment and removed the items Shona would need.

"This looks like a good fit." Falken handed Shona a pair of trousers taken from Kaspar's body. He took his knife and cut off the officer's epaulets on the shoulders. "I doubt the Marauders have any nomads in their officer corps."

Shona grinned. "Perhaps we should send Telfi."

Falken looked at Telfi, who was sitting in the IFV. The albino's skin glowed pink in the magenta interior light of the vehicle.

Both men suddenly laughed softly.

"One last item," said Falken. He took a small cannister from another compartment. He handed Shona the small stun grenade and a face mask. "Come on," said Falken. "Let's get this show on the road."

The two men shook hands, then Shona disappeared through the rear ramp.

Falken climbed into his seat and adjusted his shoulder harness. He armed the heavy .50-caliber machine gun and the .30mm cannon.

He waited five minutes and looked at his driver. "You know what to do if this turns into a clusterfuck."

The driver nodded as Falken slipped out of the IFV and was swallowed by the darkness.

★★★★★★★★★★★★★★

Chapter Forty

★★★★★★★

Shona had studied the tracks of the Marauder vehicle, noting the treadmarks had cut a groove through the perimeter patrol area. A groove that meant one thing: the vehicle was following a pattern. Or so he hoped. If that were not the case he would soon be crushed beneath the halftrack's weight.

As he lay beneath the sand where he had covered his body only moments before, he felt the ground tremble from the approaching halftrack. The vehicle drew closer.

Sticking his head out of the sand, through the eye ports of the mask he saw the side of the halftrack pass. From beneath the sand, Shona snapped to his feet, then climbed onto the back of the halftrack. Pulling the pin of the stun grenade while simultaneously opening the side door, Shona dropped the grenade into the forward cab of the vehicle and slammed the door closed.

There was a scream that was muffled by the dull sound of the grenade exploding, followed by a burst of bright light.

Climbing through the door, Shona jerked his knife from his belt and set about the gruesome task.

In less than thirty seconds the throats of six Marauders were slit from ear to ear while the men stared helplessly at the desert warrior through frozen eyes that could do nothing but watch in terror.

Shona slid behind the controls of the halftrack. He drove slowly, waiting for what he expected to see racing from the dunes at any moment.

Falken was on time. He charged from the dune and jumped through the open door. The last traces of the chemicals from the stun grenade mixed with the smell of blood and excrement; the smell stung his nostrils but he ignored the miasma.

"What about mines?" Shona asked.

"Follow the tracks. That should lead us through the minefield."

Shona eased the vehicle along the grooves until he reached a point where the tracks were less worn; tracks leading into the heart of the Marauder camp.

"There's the front door," Falken said anxiously.

The grooves threaded through what Falken suspected was the minefield, passing close to one of the hostage children. As the halftrack followed the groove, Falken looked at the child as the vehicle passed into the camp.

"It's a small boy," Falken whispered contemptuously.

Once inside the camp, Shona found another worn path. "Stay in the tread tracks," Falken suggested. "They'll lead us to something."

The tracks followed a straight line to the center of the camp. Tanks were everywhere, along with halftracks and IFV's. Sentries were more prevalent, dispersed at closer intervals.

"We're getting close to something," said Falken. "Let's hope the bastards don't stop us and make a security check."

The halftrack continued along the worn trail. Finally, Falken saw something. His eyes bulged as he stared at the vulnerable underbelly of the enemy. At the center of the camp they saw what appeared to be a mountain made of oil drums. The acrid smell of gasoline was in the air.

"Jesus. It's their fuel dump!"

★★★★★★★★★★★★★★

Chapter Forty-one

★★★★★★★★

The hardest decision Reno Falken had ever made in his life gnawed at his gut the way the stench of the gasoline gnawed at his sinus membrane. He had stood within twenty meters of the Marauder fuel depot, and giving thought to the destructive blow he could level against the enemy, he had decided otherwise.

The decision wasn't necessarily based on sound military judgement. From a military standpoint he should have tried to destroy the depot. How much destruction he might have achieved was uncertain.

What was certain was that the lives of nearly thirty hostage children would have been forfeited by that decision. That was a decision he wouldn't make. More importantly, couldn't make.

"Let's get out of here," Falken ordered. Shona turned the vehicle around and started the perilous return trip to the perimeter.

"What in the hell is that!" Falken gasped.

"One of the children."

Running in one of the deep grooves was Erica Chan. She was lit up with the physical mutation created by the prolonged freezing.

Falken slid out of the halftrack and hit the ground running. He grabbed the girl as she was about to scream, covering her mouth as he whispered, "I'm an American.

Your father is with my friends."

Falken didn't know which was her father, but he figured the words would settle the girl enough to get her into the halftrack.

She calmed down and Falken carried her into the halftrack. "Let's get the hell out of here before they discover she's missing."

Shona eased the throttle forward and the halftrack lumbered out of the camp following the grooved trail.

"Stop!" Falken suddenly ordered.

The halftrack was nearly out of the camp. It was stopped in the minefield.

"If this doesn't work . . . get the hell back to the IFV and run for Creighton's position!"

Falken pulled his knife and walked decisively through the minefield.

One step. Two steps. Three steps. Four steps.

He stopped. At his feet, the hostage child anchored to the desert stared at him with hateful eyes. "It's O.K., kid, I'm on your side," Falken whispered. He took the knife and cut the rope. He pulled the boy to his feet and turned, retracing his footsteps through the sand until he reached the halftrack.

"Let's go," Falken ordered. A stream of sweat ran down his face. The boy looked at Shona and smiled. Shona patted the boy on the head.

The halftrack sped along the grooves until it reached the outer area. At the IFV the children were transported to the American vehicle, which then raced into the night, carrying two of the hostages with it.

Two hostages that would live. The fate of the others was still up for grabs.

★★★★★★★★★★★★★★

Chapter Forty-two

★★★★★★★★

0100.

Darkness enveloped Clyde Thelan as he sat in the shadow of Roadbed Ruthie, watching a comet streak across the star-filled sky. Lieutenant Duane Barsness sat beside him, saying little while attuning his ears to the sounds of the desert. He heard a snake slither through the sand, a grating, sandpaper-type sound; then a scorpion, clicking past the perimeter of tanks formed into a defensive cocoon around Ruthie.

Thelan was a heavyset man with gray hair and brown sagging eyes. He had seen a lot for a man of forty-five. Hostile attacks on the western plains; the slaughter of his son, who was captured by hostiles while learning his father's trade. Now he was sitting in Africa, waiting for yet another attack on his beloved machine.

Barsness was twenty-two, and in many ways reminded Thelan of his dead son. His son also had been wrought-iron tough, with muscles like twists of steel. His firm jaw had been the first indicator of something he thought suspicious. Glancing at Barsness, Thelan saw the jaw set tight, then thrust out.

"Trouble?" asked the roadbed builder.

Barsness stood quickly, but catlike, and unfastened the flap on his holster. He snapped his fingers twice and two of his men sitting nearby jumped to their feet and moved quickly to their MBT's.

"I don't know. There's something out there."

"How do you know? Did you hear something?"

Barsness shook his head. "No. I felt something. A presence."

Before Thelan could say another word, there was the sharp report of a security flare piercing the air. The magnesium flare shot into the sky, then burned brightly as the parachute supporting the incendiary drifted to earth.

Through the dancing glow of the magnesium flare, there suddenly appeared a figure walking toward the bivouac.

"Thermal imaging shows one intruder, lieutenant," the voice of one of the men in an MBT shouted from the opened hatch of his tank.

A moment later, the same soldier, standing in his turret shouted, "Jesus Christ! Will you look at that ugly sucker." Then he started laughing.

The figure kept coming closer until finally, the new arrival was standing in the center of the camp.

"He must have smelled the water," said Barsness.

"I've read about them, but I've never seen one before. I didn't know any had survived the Cataclysm," said Thelan.

The tanks quickly emptied as the other soldiers hurried to see what they knew was a camel. The men walked toward the creature with caution, but soon realized there was nothing to fear.

The camel appeared harmless.

The camel, a two-humped dromedary, stood splay-legged, looking at the Americans with the same curiosity as he was being viewed.

"Get some water," Barsness ordered.

The curiosity created by the creature caused a

momentary fault in the bivouac's security. A fault keenly observed by Veries, who was watching through night vision goggles 200 yards away.

Reaching into his pocket, he removed a black plastic transmitter and pressed a button. The device was armed.

Veries was African, which meant he knew about camels. He had seen them in the veldt outside the biosphere, and killed many of them during the drive north. Camels survived the Cataclysm, he knew, because they were the most resilient animal in Africa. On a continent turned to desert, the camel, or desert schooner, as they had been called in previous centuries, had thrived and multiplied.

Another curious aspect of the camel was its digestive system. Like a cow, a camel had several stomachs.

This particular camel's stomachs, with the exception of one, were completely filled.

Filled with explosives.

Veries pressed the switch on the detonator. There was a thunderous explosion as camel parts, mixed with human parts, flew from the bivouac area.

In less than a breath, the American soldiers were dead, along with the man who operated the machine that laid the great bed of hardened liquid sand through the desert.

★★★★★★★★★★★★★

Chapter Forty-three

★★★★★★★

0200.

The Iron Horse reached the MNF's eastern position on schedule. Straddling the roadbed and track, the camp sat nestled between two mountain ranges on the north and south. Everything to the east was considered frontier. The only asset in the frontier that was considered vulnerable was the track-laying crew. Clayton had held off bringing the crew back to base in order to deceive the Marauder recon elements. He figured if the crew was spotted withdrawing it would be interpreted as a prelude to an advance.

"I hope your use of my people as bait hasn't blown up in your face, colonel," Derider said acidly.

Clayton ignored the rebuke and got on the radio to Lieutenant Barsness, but all he received was a steady hum of static.

Clayton had been a soldier most of his life; he had developed the instinct for sensing trouble before it was discovered. He felt there was trouble now.

The camp commander climbed into the control center and shook hands with Clayton. Lieutenant Colonel Anthony Wyatt was a Brit who was raised in the London Biosphere. Wyatt was tall and slim; he wore a flowing moustache and Vandyke beard. His hair and facial hair were flaming red; his eyes green and steady. He, too, looked concerned.

"We have not had a sit rep in over an hour. The SOP is to give a situation report every thirty minutes from dusk to dawn."

Clayton shook his head. "There's four MBT's out there with that track crew. I can't imagine four MBT's being taken out without a warning signal."

Wyatt thought for a moment and reached the only other conclusion. "It certainly isn't radio trouble. Not with four MBT's. The only other possibility is that the personnel have been rendered ineffective."

"Ineffective." Clayton thought about the report on Armbrust. "Do you think those bastards were able to contaminate our men with more of that virus?"

"Highly unlikely. All personnel have been ordered to avoid any suspicious people. Especially children."

"Mr. Derider, bring up the line on your computer."

Derider punched several buttons on a console. A computerized map came on the display. The map gave topographical information on the entire quadrant. A red line indicating the track bed ran east from Base Camp One through their present location and ended at end of line, indicated by a flashing red light."

Clayton studied the map. "That's about 150 miles to their location."

"The Iron Horse can cover that distance in an hour, colonel," said Derider.

Clayton shook his head. "We have to load the MNF force. That'll take at least four hours. Maybe longer. I have another idea."

Clayton took the radio and adjusted the frequency. When he reached his party he recognized Creighton's voice.

"Captain, I am relieving you from your position. You are approximately seventy-five miles from the end of track. There is a communications failure with Barsness and his patrol. I want you to take two MBT's and two IFV's and find out what the hell's happened. The remainder of your element will be temporarily attached to Colonel Forchette."

When Creighton responded, Clayton returned his attention to the map. He didn't say what was on his mind, but he did believe he already knew what Creighton would find.

"The bastards," he breathed hatefully. "The bloody bastards."

★★★★★★★★★★★★★★

Chapter Forty-four

★★★★★★★

Creighton's element had taken up a position on the eastern end of Forchette's extension; when the battle began his tanks would swing into the Marauders' rear, closing off their retreat. But first there was the mission to the end of track.

"Saddle up!" Creighton ordered Puhaly and Fergus, who were sleeping in the warm sand beneath a lean-to draped from the side of the Chariot.

Fergus came up grumbling. Puhaly came up choking. "Christ, Fergus. Don't you ever wash your feet? It smells like death warmed over in here."

Fergus farted, and left that as his reply. Puhaly started to reach for the driver, but the crafty midget was too quick. He was inside the tank and buttoned up before Puhaly could close ground.

"The little cocksucker. I'm going to tear his ears off some day," Puhaly said while stretching. Then he looked up as he heard the whine of an approaching vehicle. His hand went to his pistol, and Creighton was starting to climb the hull to get position behind the machine gun when Falken's IFV entered the bivouac area.

The IFV slid to a stop and the rear ramp lowered. The first sight to appear was Shona. He was carrying one of the hostages, a young boy. Then the girl appeared. She was wearing the Marauder blouse that had belonged to Kaspar.

"Erica!" The voice of Phillip Chan split the air. Chan and Eliason raced toward the children. Another man followed. He seemed to recognize the boy hostage.

Falken reported to Creighton. "It's not much," he said while looking at the two children. "But it's something."

Creighton's face was twisted into something of an angry mask. "You went inside that goddamned camp?"

Reno nodded.

"Of all the stupid things to do, Reno. Damn you. You could have been captured or killed. And you could have blown the whole operation."

"Fuck it," Falken snapped. "You wanted to have a recce. I got you a recce. I just happened to bring along a couple of American kids to boot."

Creighton's face softened. "Like when we were kids, huh?"

Falken loosened. "Yeah. Like when we were kids."

Creighton watched the reunion. Falken whispered, "The girl had a pretty rough go of things. I suspect she's been heavy-duty brutalized. If you get my drift."

Creighton saw Dana Macur walk and join Chan and his daughter. Creighton motioned her over.

"Take her and the boy to the field hospital. I want complete physicals. But first, see if she can tell you anything important."

Dana went to the girl; her father seemed angered that she would be interrogated, but Dana insisted. She came back a few minutes later. Her face was bone white.

"What did she tell you?"

Dana unravelled the whole gory tale of what the young girl had suffered at the hands of Veries. Creighton grew sick. His thoughts flashed back to his wife, how she had been brutalized by Benhaddou before being murdered.

At least, he thought, the girl was alive. And where there was life there was always hope.

"There was one other thing. She said Veries left the camp last night. He took an armored unit out of the camp. That's how she was able to escape his tent. She got free during his absence."

Creighton remembered the order to check the track crew. "I have an idea I know where the bastard was headed."

★★★★★★★★★★★★★★

Chapter Forty-five

★★★★★★★

0430.

"Sonofabitch!" Clayton cursed and nearly tore the microphone lead from the receiver. He turned to Derider, and the train engineer knew the answer to the question that had haunted him for over two hours.

"Hold your position," he ordered Creighton. "I'll get back to you."

"They're dead." Derider wasn't asking a question. He knew it was a statement of fact.

"Hell, yes, they're dead. And add to the list the bastards have gotten their hands on four of our MBT's."

"You callous bastard!" Derider snapped to his feet and acted as though he was going to throw a punch.

Clayton aimed a hard, warning finger at Derider. "You go easy, son. I know you're upset at losing your man. But you better remember I just lost over a dozen of mine."

Derider stormed out of the control center rather than continue the discussion. He wasn't in the mood for comparing body counts.

"Little good the MBT's are to the enemy, Colonel Clayton." Wyatt was giving the situation further thought. "What good are the tanks if they don't know how to operate them?"

"A tank is a tank, Colonel Wyatt. They might not be able to operate all the systems, but they can learn to operate *some* of the systems. That'll give them more of an edge than I care to allow."

"What makes you think they can operate some of the systems?" Wyatt suddenly looked uncomfortable.

"Because . . . the MBT's weren't hauled away toward the enemy camp. They were driven away . . . toward our position."

"Driven?"

"Yes, hell . . . driven. The buggers must have a few smart ones in their outfit. Creighton's in pursuit. I only hope he can catch up to them before they reach their objective."

"What do you think is their objective?"

Clayton nodded sarcastically. "The bastard leading the enemy has played it close to the vest. He's been laying back. There have been too many subtle hints of his presence. He knows we're aware of his presence out there on the flank. That's why the bastard hit the pyramid and took the children. Why the child Forchette found was sent in her direction. Why Kaspar led Creighton's unit into the desert, toward the pyramid. To find those people."

"Find them? For what reason?"

"So they could report back to headquarters of a large enemy offensive about to jump off on our eastern flank."

"If that's true, he would lose the element of surprise. That would be foolish. Especially when he knows our weapons are superior."

Clayton laughed. "Surprise? Think, colonel. Think. What was our immediate reaction once we learned he was on the eastern flank?"

Wyatt's moustache twitched. "What we're doing. Mounting up our forces and preparing to engage him in the desert."

"Precisely. And how are we moving our forces to the point of debarkation?"

"The Iron Horse."

"Yes. The Iron Horse. The whole force, with the exception of Forchette, which is a conventional unit with tanks similar to theirs, will be on this damned train!"

Wyatt's eyes widened. "They plan to use the missile capability on the MBT's to destroy the train. Destroy the train and he destroys your entire AfriKorps MBT's and my MNF squadron. With the exception of Creighton's and Armbrust's MBT's, and those could be worn down through mere attrition after he turns and attacks Forchette's smaller conventional force."

"That sonofabitch! He's holding his division in reserve until the train has been destroyed. Then he'll attack. That shrewd sonofabitch."

The breath was nearly out of Wyatt as he added, "He could roll up the entire continent in one bold move."

★★★★★★★★★★★★★★★

Chapter Forty-Six

★★★★★★★★

0500.

Colonel Motti listened with growing anger as an officer explained discovering the halftrack, the dead crew, and the two missing children. Their presence would certainly be known now. Soon the battle would begin.

"Two brats aren't important. They won't know anything. The others though . . . they are important." He looked at the officer. "Load the others and transport them to Veries's position. You have one hour to reach Veries." He touched a point on the map.

The officer saluted and left the tent. Motti sat in a chair and studied the map illuminated by a single lantern dangling from the center support pole.

An *X* marked the spot where Veries would be waiting for the children. East of that position was the designation for the European frontier camp.

"Now," he mumbled. "Let the Europeans come."

★★★★★★★★★★★★★★

Chapter Forty-seven

★★★★★★★

0530.

Veries and two of his men had worked furiously trying to learn the missile system of the American tanks. *Complicated. But not impossible,* thought Veries. He was impressed by the technology. He knew the tanks could literally disappear to infrared sensing; a masking system he had not yet figured out how to operate. But the forward drive of the machines was the easiest. His drivers had figured out the solar-powered system within a half-hour of taking command of the tanks from the dead Americans.

He chuckled at how easily the Americans had been deceived. What was that old saying . . . "curiosity killed the cat." In this case, it killed more than a cat.

"What about the missiles, Bofars?"

One of the more brilliant officers in his division, a lieutenant named Bofars had been studying the missile system since the capture of the tanks.

"Do you understand its operation?" asked Veries.

Bofars explained what he had learned. He pressed a switch at the gunner's console marked TIRT.

"This system operates by homing in on a target's treads. The gunner uses the GPS, the gunner's primary sight. The laser rangefinder fires an electronic beam at the target, which returns to the computer, feeding the cyclic rate of the treads into the software memory."

"Then what?" Veries demanded.

"The target is then locked-up. When fired, the missile rides on an electronic beam toward the target. Once lock-up is complete, the target cannot become disengaged unless the beam is broken by the gunner."

"What about the firing of the missiles?"

Bofars shrugged. He pointed at a switch covered by a red cowl. He flipped the cowl up. A red light appeared on the computer screen indicating the missile was armed and ready to fire. "The target itself becomes its worst enemy. Like a magnet, the target pulls the missile to its location."

"Ingenious," said Veries. "And soon we'll have these weapons. We can roll through Europe with little or no opposition."

Bofars agreed. "But first we must stop the train. If we destroy the train, we can destroy the American military. There will be a lot of destruction, but I'm certain many of the missiles will survive. And crew. Among them we will find those who can teach us the full operation of the tank's other systems."

"But for now, you feel confident you can fire the missiles at the train?"

Bofars grinned. "The train runs on tracks, not treads. There's no difference. Once we get the lock-up on the wheels of the train it will be the same as locking onto treads. Then we fire and blow the train apart. That will destroy the Americans."

"How long will it take you to instruct the others in the operation of the missiles?"

Bofars looked confident. "I can have them trained in an hour. Accuracy is no problem. The accuracy is built into the system. Since we'll be stationary and not moving, we need to only fire the missiles."

Veries checked his watch. "The lorry from division should arrive soon. Then the final preparation will be in place."

"What about the train? When will it come?"

"I have sent two scouts down the track. They travelled all night. They are well camouflaged and will warn us when the train nears their position."

"How much time will we have?"

"If the train is going as fast as I have seen it travel, we will only have fifteen minutes to prepare our reception."

"Then I better get started on the instruction. And you had better hope the train doesn't arrive early."

Veries climbed out of the MBT and looked to the east. The sun was rising but through the gray dawn he could see the approach of the lorry.

"In every battle there's the element of luck. The train won't arrive before we're ready."

He laughed a demonic laugh as he saw the cargo approach.

★★★★★★★★★★★★★★

Chapter Forty-eight

★★★★★★★

0700.

The Iron Horse glided along the freshly laid track; a high-pitched hum crackled through the early morning air, signalling the approach of the bullet-shaped train.

A hum that was barely audible to the two Marauder tanks hidden in the rocks of the mountains overlooking the valley.

The crew of the tanks were standing outside their units, some relieving themselves against the rocks; others were eating from tin cans. A Marauder officer watched through field glasses as the train streaked along the floor of the desert. He had never seen such a sight in his life.

"A pity," he said to his gunner. "Such a beautiful train. It will be destroyed in a matter of minutes."

The officer took the microphone and spoke quickly into the unit. "Veries . . . the train has passed my position. It is moving very fast. It should reach your position in approximately fifteen minutes."

From his position farther down the valley, Veries ordered, "Hold your position. I don't want your presence known by the Americans. Repeat. Hold your position."

The Marauder tanker replied in the affirmative and turned to his gunner. He accepted a can of food from the soldier. The food was rancid in taste; but he didn't seem to mind. It would get better, he told himself. When the invasion of Europe was complete they would control the lush farmland of the Continent and eat only the best food that could be grown by the Europeans, whom they would use as slaves.

Only the best. And the young women. The women he had heard of from others who had been part of the probe onto the Continent last year.

Lush young women.

He started to laugh. As he turned he saw the gunner's face suddenly stiffen. His mouth was frozen open. The food he was chewing suddenly began to spill from his mouth.

The gunner clutched at his throat and the officer thought he was choking on the food when he saw something that changed his mind.

A streak of crimson ran down his throat; there was a large hole where his Adam's apple had bobbed only moments before while chewing.

Then, the muffled sound like a child coughing. Another soldier fell. Another cough.

The officer reached for the microphone dangling from the Leopard's external radio communications console. He started to sound the alarm when he felt a piercing, burning pain through his back.

Looking down, he saw a primitive spearhead jutting through his chest.

Blood ran off the primitive spear. Turning, he saw what was the strangest sight of his life. A life that was rapidly drawing to a close.

A white-skinned man with pink eyes and white hair held a spear. On the end of the spear was a skull. Behind him, standing over the dead bodies of his soldiers, a tall black man stood triumphantly.

In his hand was a smoking pistol. Threaded onto the muzzle of the pistol was what he recognized as a silencer.

The cough!

Telfi ripped the spear from the officer's back and watched the man sink to his knees.

The chief of the Sharawi wiped the blood on the officer's tunic, then turned and grinned at Shona.

In his other hand, Shona held a radio. He pressed the switch and spoke quickly. "They are dead. The train is approaching your position."

Creighton's voice called back, "Good job. Follow the track to the train."

An IFV roared from its position a mile away and picked up Shona and Telfi. Leaving the area where the dead Marauders lay, Creighton stared hatefully at the treadmarks left by their Leopard tanks.

"They were easy to track. Weren't they, my friend?"

Telfi grinned, still wiping the blood from his spear. Then he took the spear and made a small laceration among the tangles of scars on his chest.

It was the Sharawi's way of keeping count of how many they had killed in battle.

He hoped before the day was over his chest would stream with the blood from many more such victory marks.

★★★★★★★★★★★★★★

Chapter Forty-nine

★★★★★★★

Eliason paced nervously about, watching Colonel Marie Forchette sitting calmly in a folded chair stationed outside her MBT. Unlike the other tanks in her MNF squadron, as commander she had earned the tank from Clayton for her service in the early days of the campaign. She hoped the entire MNF would ultimately have the state-of-the-art tanks, but for now they would have to make do with the French AMX-40, now solar-equipped but lacking the stealthier capabilities of the MBT's or their computerized weapons systems.

Her squadron was positioned at the end of the valley. If Clayton's plan worked, she would be the bait to spring the trap. If the plan failed, she wouldn't be alive to see the sun set.

"You look confident, colonel. I would have never thought anyone could be so calm before going into battle," said Eliason.

Forchette stood and straightened her blouse. She wore the paperlike disposable uniform of the AfriKorps.

"I'm always nervous, Mr. Eliason. That creates caution."

"I understand. It's the same with scientific research. Only in your profession, the stakes are a lot higher."

She checked her watch. "The stakes are very high at this moment. For all of us."

"Why were we brought to your location?" he asked. They had been moved from Creighton's location after TC left with his patrol.

She looked at the group of Americans from the twenty-first century. Most were sitting beside vehicles, except for Chan, who was standing with his daughter.

Forchette knew what had happened to the girl. She started to say something, but over the radio of her tank she heard the voice of Derider gasp from the Iron Horse.

"My God . . . they're on the track!"

★★★★★★★★★★★★★★★

Chapter Fifty

★★★★★★★★

On the computer inside the Iron Horse, Derider suddenly saw the thermal images of what he estimated were more than two dozen targets glowing on the display. The images were on the track. The train was travelling at over 150 miles per hour and he wasn't certain if there was enough time to stop. He pressed the control switch and felt the straps of his shoulder harness dig into his shoulders; he felt the increase of G-force as well, giving him a sick feeling in the stomach.

"They're using the children to stop the train," shouted Clayton, who instantly keyed the microphone he had been holding since the train passed Shona's position.

Ready to send the signal.

"Take them out!" Clayton ordered.

Chapter Fifty-one

Veries's lorry and four Leopard tanks sat off to the side of the four MBT's positioned on line; their turrets faced forward, toward the tracks. Bofars had done his job well, giving the other commanders a crash course in the use of the missile systems. The ambush position was north of the tracks, protected by huge boulders at the base of the northern mountain range running east along the desert.

The gunners' sights were set on the tracks; particularly, on the dark-skinned children anchored to the hardened track bed. The train would have two choices: stop for the children or run them over. In any event they would serve as an excellent target acquisition point.

"The train is coming," Veries whispered to Bofars.

That was when he heard the low, ear-splitting whine of a missile and Veries cursed because one of the damn fools had fired prematurely.

In the next instant he knew that wasn't the case. The sound of the missile was not outgoing—it was incoming.

Then the first explosion followed. Then another. A third. Looking through the periscope, Veries's eyes widened as he saw the three MBT's rupture and turn into red-hot fireballs.

In an instant they disappeared.

More rockets thundered, and he felt the tank he was sitting in rock as a projectile—not a missile, but a HEAT round—hit the treads, knocking the MBT onto its side.

His ears bled from the concussion, and looking down, he saw that Bofars had pitched over, his eyes bulging, though now lifeless.

"Shit," he cursed, trying to push open the cupola. There was another explosion, then another, and more as he quickly realized his Leopards had been destroyed.

Pushing his body through the cupola, he found himself in a cloud of smoke.

Veries realized the Americans had fired the smoke to prevent the laser rangefinder from operating, in the event that they didn't surgically remove their own MBT's as a threat to the train.

A smoke screen that might give him the momentary cover he would need to reach the lorry. The lorry had been spared. There was a radio he could use to warn Motti, who would be advancing, waiting for his signal the train had been destroyed before ordering a full-throttle charge.

His mind flashed a schematic of the area. The turret was facing toward the track. The lorry was to the left. He studied the MBT lying like a giant turtle tossed onto its side, saw the main gun, and knew which direction to take.

Through the smoke he stumbled, at times feeling on the ground with his hands. Then, through the cloud of smoke, there was the faint outline of what he knew was the lorry.

Suddenly, he stopped. There was another outline. This outline faint, but smaller.

A man! He reached for his pistol, but before he could draw and fire, a hard fist shot through the smoky curtain;

a blow that crushed his jaw and thrust him into another cloud, this one dark and swirling.

"I've been waiting for you, motherfucker!" Steve Puhaly leered at the downed Marauder.

★★★★★★★★★★★★★★

Chapter Fifty-two

★★★★★★★★

The scene at the Iron Horse was almost more than Derider could bear. On the tracks there were twenty-six children from the pyramid. They were dehydrated, nearly starved, and terrified beyond belief, which was evidenced by the change in their physical characteristics: white hair, red eyes, and dark skin.

"Get the medics up here," Clayton ordered. From the hospital platform doctors and nurses began hurrying forward with stretchers.

Clayton took the microphone and spoke with Creighton. "Did you capture one of them alive?"

Creighton's voice came back. "Yes, sir. We have the one called Veries. His jaw is sore, but he can talk."

"Good. Now get him on the radio. You know what he's got to say. Otherwise, we're going to have to change the plan. We're unloading from this point."

Creighton understood. Walking to Veries, he found the tank commander sitting on the ground beside the Marauder lorry. He was rubbing his jaw while staring spitefully at Puhaly.

The gunner stepped forward to meet Creighton. "He's not saying much, TC. Name and nothing else."

Creighton leered past the gunner to the enemy soldier. "We'll see."

Kneeling beside Veries, Creighton came directly to

the point. "You are going to contact your commander and send the signal that the train has been destroyed. Do you understand?"

Veries spit at Creighton. In a defiant voice, he said, "Go fuck yourself."

Creighton turned and motioned to another soldier from AfriKorps. Lieutenant Mike Armbrust walked angrily to where Creighton was interrogating the prisoner. He had a heavy bandage over his eye. The good eye burned with fury.

Creighton pointed at Armbrust. "This man was tortured by one of your people. Major Kaspar was his name. A thoroughly rotten sonofabitch, as I expect you are. Kaspar is dead. We captured him after he brutalized this man and killed nearly seventy of my soldiers. You're going to do as I instruct or I'm going to turn you over to him. At that point you'll be considered no longer valuable and we'll change our plans to accommodate your advancing armored division. The job will be a little more difficult, but not much. In the end we will destroy your element. Do you understand?"

Veries nodded cautiously.

Creighton continued. "Lieutenant Armbrust, tell Captain Veries what you have planned for him."

Armbrust knelt on one knee. He took out his knife and with his free hand jerked open Veries's shirt. Then he explained the painful future that lay ahead if Veries remained uncooperative.

"It's a trick I learned from the hostiles in my country. The hostiles were like the nomads in this country. Mean bastards. I'm going to stake you out naked. Right on top of that mound." He pointed to a mound rising up from the sand. The mound was tall, conical in shape.

Armbrust continued. He held up a jar of what appeared to be some sort of thick liquid. "This is honey. It's very sweet. I got the honey from the people in the pyramid. After staking you out, I'm going to rub this all over your ass, your balls, face, eyes . . . your entire body. Then I'm going to sit and watch the picnic." He put his finger in the jar and removed a bit of the syrup, touching it to Veries's mouth.

Veries tasted the sweetness, then stared at the mound. Thousands of tiny dark insects could be seen crawling around from the base to the top of the mound. He recognized the mound. And the black soldier ants crawling around. He had seen bodies devoured by the ants.

"You wouldn't!" Veries screamed.

Armbrust touched his blind eye. "I hope you don't talk. I want to hear you scream the way Kaspar made me scream." He tilted the jar and allowed a stream of the thick honey to drip onto Veries's bare stomach.

Veries flinched like a child bitten by a dog.

Creighton reached into the lorry and pulled the radio mike through the window. He held the mike for Veries. "You can talk now . . . or scream for hours. It's up to you. You give the signal—and nothing else. You warn them . . . or you go to the picnic as the main course. Do you understand?"

Veries was a practical man. He was brave to a point and could withstand pain and torture. But every man had his limits. What Kaspar did to Armbrust was bearable. What the ants would do to him was beyond comprehension.

Death would be too slow for any man to withstand.

Veries leaned into the keyed microphone. "Colonel Motti, this is Veries. The objective has been destroyed."

PART FIVE
THE CLASSIC

★★★★★★★★★★★★

Chapter Fifty-three

★★★★★★★

1400.

Colonel Motti stood in the turret of his Leopard tank, studying the cloud of dust rising to his front, a distance he judged to be less than ten miles. Lowering the binoculars, he looked down at his gunner, who watched the tank commander's face beam with satisfaction.

"The MNF force is racing for their lines. They have heard about the train. It's only a matter of time now. We'll go through the eastern outpost like shit through a goose!"

Motti's division was moving at full speed across the desert; 150 tanks charging in an on-line formation.

Motti was in the lead. He was in great spirits. *Exuberance* was the word that crossed his mind. He reached back and released an aerial. Attached to the top of the aerial was his red pennant of command; the pennant swung wildly for a moment, then steadied to a laid-back position as the tank stormed onward.

Waves of tanks followed, supported by halftracks loaded with infantry troops as well as infantry fighting vehicles to mix it up when the fighting became close.

The storm raised on the desert floor was all Clayton needed to see through his binoculars.

"Forchette's *en route*," he reported to Wyatt, whose MNF tanks were holding down the rear area.

"Send the train back down the track. Stand ready, Derider." Clayton ticked off another order without moving the binoculars from his weathered face.

"Moving to eastern station," Derider reported.

The Iron Horse hummed and began its movement to a position behind the MNF forces.

"Creighton, you and Armbrust's people prepare to swing the gate closed."

At the end of the valley, deployed behind large boulders, Creighton eyed the advancing tank division through his binoculars. The armored unit was entering the mouth of the valley. Across the valley, Armbrust was watching as well. He had four tanks under his command. Should anyone try to escape—if there was anyone left to escape—they would find the eight MBT's waiting with their deadly reception.

In her tank, Forchette was leading the charge toward Clayton's position. Moving past the end of track, she could see the track-laying equipment was still on the bed at the end of track.

In an IFV near the center of the march, Eliason was staring through an opened gunport, but all he could see was the storm of dust swirling around the vehicle and he thought he was in a tornado.

In a sense he was; a whirling, twisting cyclone created by man.

And he was saddened that mankind had learned little in the past century.

Erica Chan sat beside her father; her features were normalized, but her eyes burned with an intensity that made only one statement: she wanted to kill!

Clayton felt the same way and was prepared for just that opportunity. He had put into the field two squadrons of MBT's. The squadrons were designated Blue Squadron and Red Squadron. Each squadron was composed of four armored companies; four platoons to each company. Three platoons of MBT's supported by one platoon of IFV's. Each platoon had four MBT's with the IFV platoon having twelve infantry fighting vehicles. The squadron's fighting complement amounted to thirty-six MBT's and forty-eight IFV's.

Red Squadron was on the north flank of the railroad track; Clayton's Blue Squadron was on the south flank. Over seventy MBT's and nearly one hundred IFV's waiting to spring the trap.

Advancing at full speed was the Green Squadron commanded by Forchette. Her command had the same number as the Red and Blue Squadrons. In the rear, Wyatt sat waiting with the Gold Squadron deployed to both flanks of the tracks.

"Come on you bastards," Clayton whispered at the advancing storm of dust rising higher than the nearer storm created by Forchette's advance.

Standing in the boulders overlooking the desert floor, Shona and Telfi looked at each other. They said nothing and each sensed they were about to witness an event that would determine their fates, and the fates of their people. A fate that would be determined by men who had once been strangers. Men on both sides of the battle line.

Then they knelt, and endured what most consider the worst aspect of combat: the wait for the battle to join.

★★★★★★★★★★★★

Chapter Fifty-four

★★★★★★★

Motti passed the end of track and entered the valley, recognizing the track-laying machine described by Veries. He recalled the idea of using the camel and at the time thought the ploy stupid. Now he was certain the idea had been one of the better ones he had heard. Certainly better than Kaspar's.

The gunner's voice broke over the radio. "Colonel . . . the enemy advance is slowing."

Odd, thought Motti. They should be running headlong toward their lines. Perhaps they were choosing to stand and fight while reserves came up from the rear. No problem, he thought. That would make the battle more interesting. More costly, but certainly more interesting, and against a smaller force.

"Give me the range," Motti ordered the gunner. The gunner estimated through the stadia lines of his gunsight that the Marauders were closing fast.

"Five kilometers and we're closing."

Motti clapped his hands together, then he saw something peculiar. A second later his gunner reported the same sighting.

"The squadron has split into two elements, colonel." A pause, then, "I believe they are going to stand and fight."

Motti took his radio and called his squadron commanders. With four squadrons he had nearly 150 tanks. The Europeans would be easy pickings.

"Squadron One and Four will deploy echelon right to the north flank. Squadron Two and Three echelon left to the south flank. Engage and destroy the enemy."

In his gunner's seat, the gunner suddenly sat up straight. Through his headphones he was hearing a chirping sound.

"Colonel, something's wrong. We have laser lock on our tank!" He sounded nearly panic-stricken.

"Impossible," shouted Motti. "They don't have that range."

Then he thought of something and his eyes widened. "Veries!"

A split second later he ordered the driver, "Drop back. Drop back now, you fool."

The tank surged forward as the forward momentum began to play out and the Leopard slipped in behind another tank.

Moments later Motti realized what was happening.

"Fuck! The train wasn't destroyed."

★★★★★★★★★★★★★★

Chapter Fifty-five

★★★★★★★

"Fire!" Clayton's voice reverberated over the radio net, shouting the order every tank commander had held his breath for since boarding the Iron Horse. Lined abreast, the tanks in the front row of each squadron had target acquisition on four tanks. The computer measured distance, laser-targeted, then fired a salvo. "The 'fire and forget' SABOT rounds began finding their targets with deadly accuracy. Minutes later, the next row swept past the front row and fired four rounds.

In a matter of minutes, the Red and Blue Squadrons had killed seventy-two tanks, nearly half the attacking division.

From the flanks, Forchette's tanks opened fire, mostly targeting the IFV's darting crazily through the maze of twisted, burning hulks.

Before Motti could get into range to fire his first shot, he screamed over the radio, "Retreat!"

Breaking from the pack, Motti ordered the driver to swing right, turning into the dust storm swirling from the desert floor.

The bright-red pennant danced wildly above his tank, a pennant Clayton was watching through his binoculars.

"You bastard, I've got you now!" He looked down at the gunner, ordering "Lock-up the tank with the red pennant. One TIRT."

The gunner sighted through the GPS until he had lock-up on the treads of the tank. Pressing the computer button marked TIRT, for "tread image response tracking," the tread signature of Motti's tank was registered into the computer. Lock-on followed.

Clayton grinned. "You have just enough time to jump off that fucking tank before I send you to Hell."

If the two commanders shared mental telepathy, Motti wasn't receiving. The TIRT missile shot from the rack and streaked toward the retreating tank.

Inside, the chirping noise was driving Motti to the edge of insanity. The missile struck the treads. The tank ruptured, lifting ten feet into the air.

Motti felt his body shredded by flying scraps of metal.

The Marauder died without so much as a scream to voice his displeasure.

Without seeing the new player in the game arrive with awesome firepower and accuracy:

The Iron Horse!

★★★★★★★★★★★★★★

Chapter Fifty-six

★★★★★★★

Derider sat at the controls acquiring targets through the computer sight mounted on the nose of the Iron Horse. The track bed split the Marauder units in two, allowing Derider to fire to the front and both flanks.

Target after target was locked-up. IFV's and tanks. The IFV's and halftracks were drilled with the deadly fire of the .30mm chain gun. The "dragon flame," as he called the gun, shredded one target, then switched to the next selection on the computer menu.

Ruhland was operating the controls, watching through a periscope that played a televised account of the battle on a display above the control panel.

The rumble of a TIRT missile echoed as Derider launched another deadly missile toward the fleeing Marauders. Following its track, Ruhland saw a tank disintegrate.

But the most awesome weapon was about to take the stage.

"Keep your eye on the screen, Nick. I'm going to rain down hell from heaven."

Derider pressed several buttons, arming the multifaceted "intelligence weapons" on the fortress platform. From the train's waist, deemed the "hunter's platform," Derider sent into the sky a WISM, a multiple warhead image-seeking missile. The missile soared over the battlefield and began picking up vehicular images programmed into the computerized brain. With each target acquisition, the missile released a smaller missile, a cluster-type bomb that snaked its way through the battlefield and struck whatever target had been scanned and image-loaded into the brain.

The effect was devastating. The missile soared like a modern doomsday machine: scouting, hunting, firing cluster bombs that tore through the hulls of tanks, IFV's, all enemy vehicles, turning their interiors into a hailstorm of flying metal and shard.

On the battlefield, what few tanks that were able to fire did so with aggravating ineffectiveness. Coated with the defensive "laser-shed" exteriors, the MBT's had computers to pick up on laser-fired rounds, so that they could respond on the reciprocal line of projectile flight with an "anti-round round" that destroyed the incoming shell before it made impact.

"We're stomping their natural ass," yelled Creighton, who was buttoned up and firing from the tank commander's console.

The commo net was alive with the voices of the tank commanders, both AfriKorps and the multinationals.

The battle became a rout, with the Marauders running to the east, where yet another punishing gauntlet lay waiting.

Chapter Fifty-seven

Creighton was stationed at the rear of the battlefield, watching the slaughter unfold. He had Veries standing on the ground, forced to watch his armored division rendered to nothing but burning scrap metal.

The Marauder couldn't believe what his eyes revealed.

"Take a good, long look, Veries. This is what your people have to look forward to as we begin our push south. By the time we finish with you bastards, you'll wish you had stayed in the caves where your ancestors came from."

Veries said nothing. He could only watch.

The retreat was in full scale; what was left to retreat. The defeated army was now abreast of their position with the AfriKorps squadrons in hot pursuit. Studying the battle, Creighton leaned through the turret and spoke to Puhaly.

"Ready for a little target practice?"

Puhaly grinned and replied, "I'm locked and loaded . . . and ready to kick some ass!"

Creighton winked. "Then trip the lights fantastic!" Before the first round fired, Creighton spoke to his young counterpart across the valley. "Armbrust, you may begin firing."

The Chariot roared with the first salvo. A direct hit on a target at 2,000 meters. The tank's turret was ripped from the hull and spun wildly through the air.

Armbrust's MBT's opened up from the opposite side, joining in on the carnage.

Creighton walked to the rear of the Chariot. Veries was holding his hands over his ears. Creighton pulled the Marauder's hands away. "Listen to the noise, you bastard. Listen to the sound of victory!"

There was a mean look on Creighton's face. A look Veries recognized: the look of victory!

Veries had worn the same mask, only his victory was over raggedy-assed nomads, not well-trained, well-equipped, battle-hardened veterans.

In his gunner's seat, Puhaly fired another HEAT round. He reached overhead and marked another slash on a pad he had clipped to the edge of the cupola. Twelve slashes marked the paper. He then leaned down and called to Fergus, "Fergus, you little shitass, this is more fun than fucking."

"How would you know? You ain't ever been laid."

Puhaly ignored the rebuke. Not even his little nemesis Fergus could spoil the mood he was in. He started humming an old tune he had heard in the music library at the biosphere. He didn't know the name of the singer, but the tune was sweet. He had forgotten the words to the song, except the part about " . . . I left my heart . . . in San Francisco . . ."

Another round fired. He clapped his hands and scratched another slash onto the paper.

Another round. Another slash. All the while humming the tune.

He paused in the middle of the tune, sighted another tank, and fired. As the tank exploded, he said to Fergus,

"My little man, it don't get no better than this."

Everyone agreed, except Veries, who was growing sicker by the moment.

Creighton found great joy in that.

★★★★★★★★★★★★★

Chapter Fifty-eight

★★★★★★★

The aftermath of battle is where the exhilaration fades quickly into a somber, sobering reality; a reality that takes away much of the ecstasy of victory. Perhaps that's by natural design, thought Clayton. At least, among civilized people.

He didn't necessarily consider the Marauders civilized, though he did consider them human. But he was presented with a unique problem: what to do with the captured and wounded?

He knew what treatment he could expect from the enemy were the shoe on the other foot. And the thought had crossed his mind as he rode along the floor of the desert, perusing the destructive power unleashed in the last hour.

His men had been murdered, tortured, and poisoned; innocent children had been kidnapped, turned into messengers of death, brutally raped, and treated in the most inhumane fashion.

Such conflicts never existed in the DESFOR; not emotional conflict over the treatment of the captured enemy. There was policy for that situation; policy decided by the government. Here, he was the government, and was faced with a human dilemma.

Clayton switched on the radio to the frequency of the Iron Horse. "Derider, get your train out here. I want your medical personnel to treat the wounded. Have an infantry unit begin policing up those who aren't wounded."

He ordered the MBT driver to turn to the north flank where he knew a certain tank commander would be waiting. Despite Creighton's feelings toward him, he considered the boy to be like his son. Perhaps someday they might talk about that. He might tell Creighton how his father had really died. What a rotten sonofabitch he truly was.

And he truly was.

But not the mother. Clayton took a faded photograph from his pocket and studied the two faces of the woman and child seated in the Vegas Biosphere. He always looked at the picture, remembering the woman, and now, about to congratulate the son; he knew he had much to say but would probably never have the right.

Creighton would probably always hate him for what happened to his wife. Perhaps he should; maybe that would be good for him. Hate could be an asset, especially in war time.

Clayton's MBT rolled to a stop in front of Ribald's Chariot. The crew was standing around, still wearing the glow of victory.

Creighton saluted.

"Congratulations, sir. You gave us our first major victory."

Clayton took TC's extended hand. "Beats the hell out of drilling lightbulbs, sir," said Puhaly.

"You men did a fine job." He swept his arm toward the valley. "The entire unit did a fine job. And you'll be pleased to know we'll be moving downrange in the near future."

That was good news. If they were going to be in a war zone, the crew of the Chariot, like other crews, wanted to fight. Sitting on their asses was no fun.

"What about Armbrust?" asked Creighton. "Will you send him back to the United States?"

Clayton shook his head. "He can stay as long as he is capable."

"He's capable. He knocked out a group of tanks. Not bad for a man with one eye."

"Not bad at all," Clayton replied. He turned and looked at Veries. "Is this the man?"

Creighton motioned Veries to the colonel. He stood ramrod straight and saluted.

"Don't salute me, you sonofabitch! I'm taking your men prisoner. They'll be shipped to Europe where they'll be prisoners of war until this war is over. That way they'll be out of our hair. But not you. You are going to stand trial for war crimes. I know what you did to those children." He leaned into Veries's face. "Especially that young girl. I ought to let her father have you. But I can't. I'd like to kill you myself, but I can't do that either. But if you're found guilty I'll personally put the noose around your neck and hang you myself. That's the civilized way of doing things."

Veries stiffened. He started to say something but kept his mouth shut.

The Americans looked up as an IFV approached. Falken was standing in the opened turret. He looked like a knight returning from a successful day at the joust. He saluted crisply.

A second IFV rolled alongside Falken; the rear ramp opened and the figure of Dr. Carl Eliason appeared.

He was visibly shaken and appeared ready to vomit. Dana Macur followed; she had smudges of gunpowder and dust caking her face.

Veries backed away as he recognized another of the people in the IFV.

Erica Chan walked with her father. He knew the

Marauder was the man who had raped his daughter and he started forward. He was carrying a rifle.

Creighton stepped between the two men. "Put down the gun, Mr. Chan," Creighton ordered.

"Please, old friend," pleaded Eliason. "Do as he says. You will regret this for the rest of your life. He'll be punished. But not like this."

Veries edged closer to the MBT. His eyes were jerking from one American to the other. He was terrified, and in that moment of terror, did not see the person who had slipped from the group and made her way around the back of the MBT.

"I was only following orders," Veries pleaded. "You understand orders, don't you colonel?"

Clayton spit. "I understand orders. I just don't always understand the people who carry out the orders."

Veries was against the hull of the MBT when he felt a presence. He turned in time to hear a voice shout a name.

Then he saw the girl standing there, her skin dark, her hair white, her eyes as red as blood.

In her hand she held a bayonet.

Then he felt the sharp sting in his throat and saw the blood spill into his hands. The blood was the same color as the girl's eyes.

Veries slumped to the ground, sliding along the hull. Collapsing into the tread of the tank, he felt the life flowing out of his body.

The girl became blurred by the cloud now forming in his brain. But he did see one thing clearly: she had changed.

Her hair was long and dark; her skin was the color of the honey Armbrust had poured on his stomach. And her eyes were a soft brown.

She appeared to be smiling.

★★★★★★★★★★★★★★

Epilogue
Hamp's Farm

★★★★★★★★

Captain Abraham Creighton stood with the crew of Ribald's Chariot at the graveyard where his wife lay buried. The dead AfriKorps and MNF soldiers killed in the battle were laid to rest with traditional military honors.

"Taps" was played for the Americans; the "Marseillaise" for the French. The Brits had not suffered a casualty.

Creighton placed a batch of fresh flowers on Silver's grave; the cactus rose, planted there by Hamp Floris after her funeral, was still growing. But he had been given a batch of carnations, offered by Hamp at his thriving greenhouse, and he laid them at the base of the cactus rose.

After a few quiet minutes he went to where everyone had gathered for something of a farewell party.

Hamp's Farm, as it was being called, was spread over thirty acres. Rows of trees transplanted into the soil were growing beneath the sun, fed by irrigation ditches etching the earth like tank grooves worn into the ground by tank treads.

The mood was festive. The 21st Centurians, as they were now called, were leaving that afternoon, returning by ship to the United States. It was thought by the medical personnel that their "condition" could be reversed.

Creighton was standing by a table that sat beneath a

tent on the farm. Hamp was busy pouring a concoction he had made from some of the fruit trees that began bearing fruit during the trip across the ocean.

"Not bad," said Creighton, who drank the sweet liquid. "What's it called?"

"Lemonade," Floris replied. "Soon, you can drink it by the pitcher."

"Perhaps you might like something a little stronger, captain."

Creighton looked up to see Eliason approaching. He carried a bottle. The bottle was dusty. After Creighton drained his glass, Eliason recharged it with a pour from the bottle.

Creighton sniffed the liquid. It was darker than the lemonade, but had a nice smell.

"What's this?" he asked.

"Aberlour scotch. Probably the oldest on the planet. I took it along on my journey from yesterday."

Phillip Chan looked at the bottle in amazement. He stretched out his glass. "I had completely forgotten."

The three men sipped the scotch. Creighton nearly choked, and Eliason remembered something. "My God . . . I'll bet that's your first taste of the Devil's Brew."

Creighton's eyes rolled slightly, then refocused. He started to speak but his tongue grew thick.

"I believe the lad is drunk," Chan giggled. He, too, was showing the effects after falling off his century-plus wagon.

Eliason looked at the bottle. He handed it to Creighton. "Keep this, captain. It's a part of the past you never knew. One we may never know again. I'd like to know it's in the hands of someone who stands up for the good things on this earth."

Creighton detected the sadness in his voice. He

started to say something but paused as Dana moved into the group and casually slipped her arm through Eliason's. There was a glow on her face.

Creighton uncorked the bottle and reached out. He poured a healthy blast into each of their glasses until the bottle was empty.

"In that case you all deserve to share this with me." He raised his glass and toasted, "To all of us . . . the people who stand up for the good things on this earth."

They drained their glasses and giggled again. Creighton started to say something, but before he could, Eliason thrust his hand to Creighton. A hand that seemed to cross through time. Through more than a century.

Creighton gripped Eliason's hand. It was a firm handshake. And despite the things he had said to the 21st Centurian, he was glad the man had missed out on the ride through the Cataclysm.

Glad that people like him were going to be here to remind the world of what can happen when the caretakers of the earth neglect their duty.

BILL DOLAN is the pseudonym of an author who lives in North Dakota. He is a Vietnam veteran and has written several previous novels.